A Beloved Sin

Danielle Paquette-Harvey

1984 –

Cover by Jennifer Givner

ISBN 978-1-7388313-3-3 (paperback)

First Edition: March 2022

Published by: Danielle Paquette-Harvey

http://daniellephauthor.com

https://www.instagram.com/daniellephauthor

Subscribe to my mailing list so you don't miss anything!

daniellephauthor.com

Follow me
- Facebook: Danielle Paquette-Harvey author
- Instagram: daniellephauthor

Other books by the author

All my books are available on Amazon, in most libraries Barn & Nobles, and other good libraries.

Prequel to this series
- The prophecy - *ISBN 978-1777572105*

Origins
- The Goddess's Wards - *ISBN 978-1-7782178-8-3*

Longing mates Series

1. Age-Old Enemies - *ISBN 978-1777572136*
2. A Beloved Sin - *ISBN 978-1777572150*
3. The Fallen - *ISBN 978-1-7782178-5-2*

Blood and Kisses Series
  1. Cursed King – coming soon

Half-angel's daughter Series
  1. Devoured by Darkness – coming soon

Charity books

- A Wicked Taste of Fate – An Anthology -
  ISBN 978-1-7782178-6-9

  Please note: This dark fantasy anthology book contains eight short stories from different authors. All the profits go to Ste-Justine's, a children's hospital in Montreal.

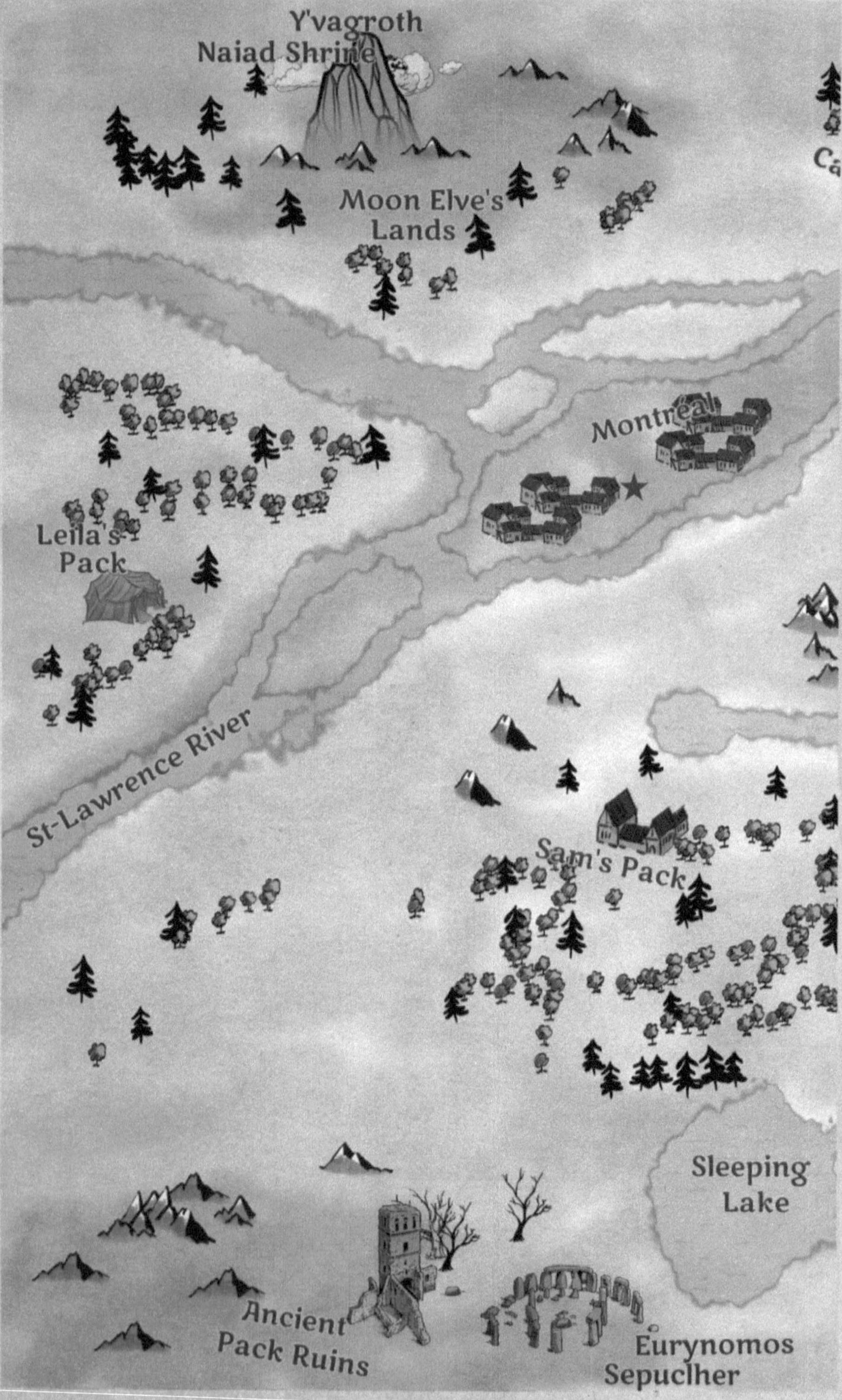

Y'vagroth
Naiad Shrine
Moon Elve's Lands
Montréal
Leila's Pack
St-Lawrence River
Sam's Pack
Sleeping Lake
Ancient Pack Ruins
Eurynomos Sepuclher

Moon Goddess Shrine
Delos
abin
Melian Nymph Sacred Grove
Valley of Nysa
Chalet
Vampire's Castle

Ladon – The Legendary Dragon
Made by the amazing Charles M. Allen
@c.m_allen

Danielle Paquette-Harvey

A Beloved Sin

Prologue (Eurynomos)

I stared at the Styx for a moment, watching the tormented souls ride on the ferry, getting across the muddy black river. The sound of their lamenting was music to my ears. Crossing the river was the only way for the cursed souls to reach the underworld. Charon, that old, emaciated skeleton, was the ferryman. He oversaw crossing the souls, but also made sure they paid the fee. Some of them tried to swim across the river but died in its poisonous water. I loved how the souls who didn't have a coin to pay had to wander the shores for one hundred years. Their despair and agony from the wait were delightful to watch. What's even better, is at the end of this wait, their tormenting and punishment were only beginning. I rejoiced with pleasure from these thoughts.*

The sound of the anvils got me out of my thoughts. I turned to look at my workers. The orcs were forging weapons, smashing the metal with their heavy hammers, sweat dripping down their foreheads. The sparks of the metal-on-metal were lighting the dark cave in Tartarus. Little further, other workers were pouring liquid metal into molds with bare hands, as a punishment for greater sins. The air was hot, and the scent of ashes was omnipresent.

I looked at my magical portal, standing not far in front of me. The bronze pillars of the portal were firmly anchored in the ground. The portal's doors looked like flowing lava, glowing red. Screaming faces were appearing and disappearing randomly, as lost souls tried to travel across it to flee the Underworld but couldn't. Although it might seem that the portal was open, I knew it was sealed. No one could come in or get out. The wretched Moon Goddess made sure of that ages ago.

I couldn't wait to crack open that damned gate! Some wizard goblins were casting their magic on it, trying to break it open, so that our army could cross into the world of the living. It had already begun. Slowly, I could see the seal of the gate weakening. Soon, my army could flood the world of the living. They would prepare everything for my coming. After all, it shouldn't be long before I can join them. When that happens, I will rule over all!

I watched as my army was gearing up for war. The raw strength of the centaur's horse's body was strong enough that they needed nothing but a pike. Harpies were diving and practicing their *sharp talons on the goblins who were too tired to flee. Those swift creatures were particularly vicious, cruel, and violent with their victims. I loved how they tortured people when bringing them into Tartarus.*

My orcs would soon be armed and armored, and the goblins were preparing their arsenal of bombs and flying machines. My army stretched as far as the eye could see. That's not even counting my lower demons. They would be willing to do anything to try to earn a place higher in ranks. Even if that wretched bitch sealed a part of my power, with a force this strong, nothing will be able to stop me!

Chapter 1 (Will)

Luna

I looked at myself in the mirror while placing my hair. I checked that my shirt was correctly buttoned. Today was an important day, and I wanted to look the part. It was the day I would present my Luna to the pack. I felt nervous and excited at the same time.

I tried to fend off this moment as much as I could. I was hoping to find my fated mate. I mean, a lot of wolves still hadn't found their fated mates at twenty-three years old, but I still had hoped to find her. I had been the Alpha for two years already. It was my duty to take care of the pack. Responsibilities were great, and it was time I settled on a Luna to help.

In the last few weeks, the pressure from the pack's advisors was growing more and more. They began talking about matching me with every single she-wolf they could find. They tried to set me up on dates to which I didn't want to go. They tried to introduce young women to me, hoping I would fall in love. It was useless and annoying. Before they went any further, I told them I had found a Luna. It wasn't true. I just told them that to get them off my back. It overjoyed them to learn I had a mate and couldn't wait to meet her! I secretly began searching about who would be a great Luna. I only had a few days to do so. I've had a few dates in the past. I loved having a woman in my arms. I thought they were deliciously perfect. But I never really found someone I'd be willing to spend my life with.

The woman I choose would not only be my Luna, but also be my mate. Even if it wasn't a fated mate, werewolves usually mated for life. She would have to be my everything. I really wanted to choose the right female. It was hard…

My sister was luckier. She found her fated mate two years ago. It was the most unexpected mate ever! I mean, who knew she would be mated to a vampire? It took some time to accept it. Eventually, everyone came around. Even me… Damien was a good guy; he was a good mate for Kate. The two of them were so in love, you could feel that nothing could bring them apart! This was the bond I had hoped to find. This unconditional love, an unbreakable bond, decided by the Moon Goddess herself.

Today, Kate has become the Queen of the vampires. Her mate, Damien, became the vampire Lord shortly after some vile succubi killed his father. She went to live with him at the vampire's castle. In fact, that's how I became next in line to become the Alpha. Kate was supposed to be the Alpha of the pack, since she's older than me by two years. I always thought I had time to find my mate, since I was destined to be a trusted Beta, defender of the pack, and leader of the attack force. But when she became the vampire Queen, suddenly, I was next in line to become the next Alpha.

Still, my father was the Alpha, until… On the day of Kate's wedding, my father mysteriously fell sick. We were all enjoying the moment. Vampires and werewolves united to celebrate a love everyone thought impossible. Age-old enemies making peace and accepting one another.

Everything was going well when suddenly, my youngest sister, Bianca, raised from her seat to warn us that Eurynomos was trying to open a gate to come into our world. That wretched demon! We were all shocked by what she had told us. Suddenly, my father, Sam, fell to the ground. He was a strong

Alpha and wasn't old yet. He was in good health, so it really came as a surprise to everyone. We rushed to him while my mother screamed. Nobody could wake him up. Steven and I brought him back home in our arms. My mother called every sorcerer and doctor from all the wolves' packs and vampire's kingdom. We even tried to call human doctors. Alas! Two years have passed, and he still rests in his bed. We were unable to cure him or to wake him up. I was declared the Alpha of the pack one month after Kate's wedding.

I jumped as someone knocked on the door. I hadn't realized I had been so deeply lost in my thoughts. I opened the door and saw Bianca. She had her long blond, almost white hair braided on the side. Her deep ice-blue eyes stared at me with affection.

"There you are," she said, smiling with open arms.

She hugged me tight, and it warmed my heart. I loved my little sister dearly.

"You know it's almost time, right? Are you ready?"

I looked at my watch. How did time pass so fast without me noticing? I smiled, embarrassed, as I rubbed the back of my head.

"Thanks for letting me know, sis. I wouldn't want to be late."

Bianca giggled.

"Especially since you're the one making the big announcement, silly!"

I giggled back at her.

"Yes, I guess you're right. Is Mom there yet?"

She shook her head.

"I'll go get her, then," I answered.

Bianca nodded. "Okay, I'll wait for you with the others."

I hugged my sister and watched her go, her long green dress hugging her feminine curves. I had to remind myself that my young sister was now twenty-two; she wasn't a kid anymore. She also had found her fated mate, our cousin Steven. It was a surprise to everyone. But we discovered that Bianca doesn't share the same genes as us. We found out she's the Moon Goddess's daughter. She's got some of the goddess's powers inside of her. She even brought Damien back to life during the war! Which was so amazing to watch! I wondered what other powers were hiding inside of her. I guessed she didn't even know herself.

I walked up to my parent's room. The room was silent and dimly lit. As usual, my mother was at my dad's bedside, reading a book. She barely ever went out anymore. She spent her days watching over my father. My parents were fated mates. Ever since my father became sick, my mother had been watching over him. I could see how much she loved him. I always thought it was great that she could feel the mate bond, even though my mother was human and my dad was a werewolf.

I looked at my dad lying in bed. He had become so thin. He was only a shadow of the man he used to be. He used to be a powerful wolf, respected by all. He could fight off anyone who would dare to challenge him. His skin was now white. You could almost see through it. He lost so much muscle mass that you could see the shape of his bones through his skin. Seeing him like that filled me with sadness. I had to remind myself that we were doing all we could to cure him, even though no one seemed to know what ailment he was suffering from.

I looked at my mother, still beautiful after all those years. A few wrinkles here and there were beginning to show. She was a devoted mother and loving wife. I only hoped that I would be lucky enough to have a partner that would love me that much.

My mother was so concentrated on her book that she didn't even notice me entering. She loved werewolf romance novels and read them all the time. Maybe it was because she knew werewolves were real. Perhaps it was because, in her way, she lived her own werewolf romance when she met my dad.

I walked up to her and put my hands gently on her shoulders from behind. She startled at my touch and raised her eyes, then calmed down and smiled as she realized it was me.

"Oh, Will! Don't scare me like that!" she scolded me.

I laughed a little, as I knew she wasn't really angry.

"It's time," I told her softly.

My mother rose to her feet and grabbed my hands in hers. They were warm and strong. She looked into my eyes, even though she was a head smaller than me. Her hazel eyes were full of worries.

"Are you sure you're making the right choice?" she asked anxiously.

I might be an adult, but mothers always worry. I smiled reassuringly and nodded.

"Jane is one of my best friends. We grew up together, and we're very close. She's my confidant. I know she'll make a good Luna."

My mother shook her head.

"But a friend is not the same as a mate. She might be your best friend, but she's not your lover."

I sighed. She was right. But Jane was the closest to a lover I ever had. I really cared about her opinions. I wanted to ensure she was all right and enjoyed spending time with her. I had known her ever since I was a child. She had been my best friend. Now that I had to choose a Luna, I figured it would only be a small step from best friend to a lover.

"You know I need a Luna. And it's not like I can afford to wait forever to find my fated mate. Jane will make a great mate for me. I've seen her soul. She's pure and gentle."

When I became the Alpha, I went to see Ayanna, the Melian nymph Queen. Like she did for all our previous Alphas she helped awaken my inner power. It seemed that I have the power to see the color of people's souls. Knowing if they're good or evil, strong or weak, just by looking at them, judging from the color and the size of their souls.

Sarah nodded.

"If that's what your heart desires," she simply said.

"It is. Please don't worry about me, Mom."

We walked together, arm in arm, to the front of the pack's house. Every member of the pack, whether wolf or human, was already there. Even my sister Kate and her mate Damien flew from the vampire's castle to be there. They were watching, front row, smiling.

Everyone stopped talking as I arrived. An Alpha was respected, and no one dared to speak unless I told them to. I was happy that my presence was held in respect by the pack. I nodded to my mother to go forth.

She took a few steps further and began talking.

"My dearest friends and family, today, we celebrate the union of two very important people. This is the day you've been waiting for. The day my son, Will, your Alpha, finally found his mate."

People started cheering in the crowd, forcing my mother to stop talking and wait. I smiled; I was happy to be loved by my pack. I believed in helping each other and getting their trust and friendship, rather than ruling by fear and force.

My mother seemed so calm in front of everyone, in control of the situation. She was used to doing speeches. She had been the Luna for many years, at my father's side. The fact she was a human didn't seem to bother her one bit.

But me? I might have seemed calm on the outside, but inside, I had a storm going on. Was this the right choice? Should I have waited for my fated mate? Will I regret this? So many questions!

After a few seconds, the crowd became silent again. My mother gave me the signal. It was time.

I opened the pack's house door. There she was, waiting for me.

Jane was prettier than ever. Her curly red hair was flowing down her shoulders. She wore a tight short peach dress. The same one she wore on our prom night. She didn't have any extravagant jewels or anything; she didn't need it either. She was beautiful just the way she was. She looked at me nervously.

Suddenly, all my doubts disappeared. She might not be my fated mate, but she will be a great mate for me. Even though she was just a common wolf in the pack. I never really cared for titles, anyway. She was a trustworthy friend, an honest woman, the sweetest one I knew.

I smiled at her as I grabbed her hand and whispered to her, "It's going to be fine."

She smiled back at me; her stress level seemed to lower a little.

Together, we arrived in front of everyone. I announced with a strong voice. "I present to you, your Luna, Jane."

The crowd cheered and applauded. Some people threw leaves and flowers in the air, for good luck. I felt so proud to stand there with Jane by my side.

People made way for Jane's parents, who were approaching. Since their daughter was now the Luna of the pack, they were getting higher in rank as well. They hugged their daughter and went behind us, by my mother's side.

Everyone's eyes were on us. I knew what needed to be done next. I had to mark her. This mark would last forever. Making sure every wolf knew she was mine. It was very intimate and important. It was tradition to do it as the she-wolf became the Luna if it wasn't already done before.

I got close to Jane. She leaned into me, presenting her neck, closing her eyes. I smelled the sweet scent of her skin. She had put on perfume and smelled like flowers. I let my lips brush against her skin, earning a small groan from her as I passed the spot where the neck meets the shoulder. That's where I needed to mark her to make her mine.

I really wanted to do this, but somehow, I couldn't grow my teeth. My wolf didn't want to come out. I didn't feel the urge to bite her, and I couldn't understand why. But I didn't want to force this on myself. If my wolf wasn't ready, then I would wait for him to be ready. At the same time, I couldn't leave like that. I felt everyone's stare weigh on my back. They wouldn't be happy if I didn't mark her and might not accept her as their Luna otherwise.

I settled for the next best thing. I decided to bite her with my human teeth. I didn't go deep through the skin as I would with my werewolf teeth. It wouldn't leave a permanent mark, as with my werewolf teeth. But it had the desired effect; Jane gasped as she grabbed by arm while I bit her and made a hickey on her neck. I continued for a few seconds, while everyone applauded, before I released her neck. I smiled as I spotted the red hickey on her white skin.

The pack's advisors had a knowing look on their faces. They knew I hadn't bitten her. I couldn't fool them. They were close enough to see, as well as Jane's parents and my mother. They kept a straight face, not showing anything. The crowd was far enough. They were fooled and thought I had bitten her. That was exactly what I needed; for everyone in the pack to think of Jane as their Luna and to trust her. The fact I hadn't marked her didn't change anything to me. She was my Luna, and I wanted everyone to respect her.

I looked into Jane's eyes. She had a complete incomprehension look on her face. She knew very well I hadn't bitten her. I didn't want her to say anything, or the crowd to see the look on her face. I grabbed her chin with my hand and brought her lips to mine. We shared a passionate kiss, our tongues dancing together. I held her close to me with my other hand while she grabbed my shoulders. My heart was racing.

When we broke the kiss, I whispered to her, "I love you."

She smiled as she answered, "I love you, too."

It was usually tradition for the new Luna to meet everyone. I didn't want to take the risk that anyone in the crowd would notice there was no mark on her neck, so we went back inside the pack's house immediately after. The pack's advisors found a reason for us not to go meet everyone, saying we were busy preparing to defend ourselves against Eurynomos.

When the advisors and our parents came inside the pack's house, the door was closed. After checking there were no prying ears, the advisors made it clear they were unhappy with me not marking my mate.

One advisor spoke first.

"Why didn't you mark her?"

They didn't even wait for my answers. They all started shouting questions.

"What will everyone think?"

"Do you love her?"

"What if the people find out?"

Their questions annoyed me. They didn't have to know. It was my choice alone.

"That is none of your business."

"But it's tradition," another continued.

I snarled at him, "As the Alpha, I make my own decisions."

They took a step back.

Then Jane started, with a small voice, "But Will..."

I could feel she was nervous to ask, and I didn't want to talk about it in front of everyone. I didn't let her finish her sentence. I lowered my tone; I knew I had been harsh with the advisors. But she was my Luna; I wanted to be nice to her, as she deserved and as her mate should be.

"Not here, Jane, come," I told her softly while brushing my thumb on top of her hand.

The advisors started to protest, "But,"

I turned to them and said in a harsh tone, "I will not hear anything more."

With that being said, I gently took Jane by the hand and led her to my room… Well, our room. It was at the far end of the pack's house, on the second floor. It was the biggest room in the house. It was modestly decorated. I didn't like luxurious things, diamonds, or bling. We had a big comfortable bed and a small fireplace. We needed nothing more to be happy. At least, that's what I thought.

I remembered that Jane liked lilies, so I had asked Bianca and Steven to get a few bouquets and set them in my room. They went a little overboard, and my room was now full of lily bouquets. All the tables and dressers had one. You could even smell the flowers without opening the door.

On one side of the room were Jane's things. Her parents had brought her stuff earlier so that she would have everything she needed to settle down into her new home.

Jane gasped as she entered the room.

"Oh wow! You remembered I love flowers!"

I smiled at her.

"Of course I did! You liked them ever since you were little. I wanted you to be happy, to feel welcome in your new home."

I took one of the white lilies and offered it to her. She giggled as she took it.

"Like when I turned seven."

I laughed, "Yes, you remember!"

"Of course I do! It was my birthday, and you offered me a lily. It was the first time someone offered me a flower. That made it much more special."

"Well, today's the start of a new beginning for us, so it's special too."

"Yes, you are right," she answered with a big smile. She looked truly happy.

She entered the room and looked at everything. Opening the drawers, the closets. Getting to know the room we now shared.

When she was satisfied enough, she sat on the bed and looked at me.

"Then… why didn't you mark me? Don't you love me?"

I could see that she was worried. I sat beside her on the bed.

"I wasn't ready to mark you. My wolf wasn't ready. I need a little more time for our relationship to grow deeper. I think my wolf still needs to adapt to everything that's happening."

She shook her head.

"You know your wolf would be ready faster if you marked me, and he got to meet with my wolf."

"You know our wolves have already met, Jane."

She nodded.

A few years earlier, on a party night with friends, we had both drank a little too much. We ran together in the woods, away from the others, and started making out. At that moment, I saw a flicker of golden in her eyes, and I knew it was her wolf coming to meet mine. I felt my wolf wanting to meet her, so I let him take the front place in my mind and greet her. The two of them stared at each other, and got to know one another while we were making love. It was an intense feeling, and I still remember it to this day. Everything just felt so real, my animal's instincts taking control of my body and heightening my senses.

Yet, to this day, I haven't felt the same with anyone. My wolf hasn't wanted to come out to meet another girl. I haven't felt the urge to mark anyone.

"You have to believe me when I say I love you, Jane. But right now, I'm not ready to mark you."

Jane sighed as she rested her head on my shoulder.

"But you know you'll have to mark me if we're to have pups, eventually."

I shrugged my shoulders. I knew she was right. I had to bite her, so she got into heat. But I wasn't in a hurry to have pups.

"Are you that eager to have some?"

She raised her head and looked me in the eyes, her green eyes studying me while she pondered.

"Not that much, but... at the same time, you are the Alpha. And the Alpha needs to have descendants to succeed them at the head of the pack."

I sighed. So many responsibilities came with being Alpha. I always tried my best to respect all the traditions and duties that I have. It was something I considered very important. But having pups was not a *duty*. I refuse to see it like that. I wanted to have pups one day, my own family, kids, laughing and running in the house. But I wanted to wait until I was ready. I wanted to have some because we wanted to, and out of love, not out of responsibilities.

I shrugged my shoulders, "it's not like I'm going to die soon. We have time to make pups."

She didn't seem satisfied with my answer and pouted her lips a little but answered, "I guess."

I could sense that she held great feelings for me. I knew I loved her, but I didn't know if I could return as strong feelings as she held for me. I had the impression that something was lacking. But I couldn't put my finger on *what*. I wondered if maybe my wolf just needed some time to adjust. I was sure that our two wolves would adapt to one another.

In the meantime, I really wanted Jane to be happy, and I really wanted to try to make this work.

I hugged her in my arms, feeling her heartbeat against mine, whispering in her ear.

"Jane, you are my best friend. We've known each other for so long. Please give me a little bit of time. I swear I will be there for you."

She relaxed in my arms, not answering anything, just enjoying the moment.

I kissed her sweetly. It was still afternoon, and we still had plenty of time before our honeymoon. And even though I didn't mark her, I had the intention of taking good care of her. I was really looking forward to this. I would have liked to stay in bed with her all day and give her all that I am, but I thought she would probably want to visit her new home.

"How about I show you around while we wait for nighttime to come?"

She smiled, knowing very well what I meant.

"That sounds like a great idea."

Chapter 2 (Bianca)

Angelus Hyssopus

Well, this afternoon didn't happen exactly as I had expected it! I knew Jane was the Luna my brother chose, but I was expecting him to hold up to the tradition and mark her. He usually has a strong sense of duty. I was puzzled as to why he didn't… I trusted my brother; he must have his reasons not to. I guess I'll have to ask him when I have the chance.

For now, I had other things to take care of. My main concern was to find a way to break that stupid curse that linked me to that wretched demon. I was so tired of watching and hearing Eurynomos all the time! At least I took comfort in the fact it had the benefit of letting me know the progress of his plans. And from what I saw of it, it was quite scary. I hoped dearly he wouldn't succeed.

"Bianca?"

I turned around to see my sister Kate smiling. Her hazel eyes seemed to glow, and her brown hair was braided, letting her emerald earrings show. She didn't wear a lot of jewelry, even though she was now the vampire's Queen and could choose to wear whatever she wanted. Damien was at her side, his long hair neatly tied in a low bun, wearing his usual jeans and shirt. I've seen him dress formally only when his title as the vampire Lord required it. I liked the fact he remained himself, even after ascending to the throne.

"Hi, Kate! Hi Damien!"

I hugged them tightly. The two of them were smiling at me. Damien's canines were slightly showing even though he didn't need to feed.

Two strong arms encircled me from behind. I knew without looking it was Steven. I might not be a werewolf and have an advanced sense of smell, but I could recognize my lover without looking.

"Hi, baby," he said while landing a kiss on my cheek. "Hi Kate, hi Damien! I'm so happy that you guys could make it," he added.

"We actually have something important to tell you!" my sister said excitedly.

"Really? What is it?" I asked.

Damien put his arm around my sister's waist affectionately. Kate rested her hand on her flat stomach.

"We're going to have a baby!" she almost screamed out of excitement.

"Oh! This is so great!!" I jumped in and took my sister in my arms.

"Congratulations!" Steven said as he shook Damien's hand.

"When are you due?" I asked them.

"We've only just found out, so it's still going to be a few months. It should be around spring or early summer," Kate answered, smiling.

"I think I've never seen a werewolf-vampire baby…" Steven pondered.

Damien chuckled at his comment.

"Neither did we. But ancient records say werewolf-vampire hybrids are very powerful, born with the powers of both races. I guess we'll find out, eventually. The only thing that matters to me is that we have a healthy baby. I don't care about the rest," he finished while hugging my sister lovingly.

"Does everyone know?" I asked.

My sister shook her head. "We're telling everyone today. But Damien's mom and Arius already know. They were thrilled when we told them!"

"Anyway, we wanted to ask you guys to come back to the castle with us," Damien added.

I looked at him with wondering eyes. He continued without waiting.

"Elwin found some new books on demons in the library. You might be able to find something about Eurynomos. He also wants to show some herbs that he hopes will help your father."

That sounded very interesting! I was out of fresh ideas on both topics, so I would gladly take all the help I could from anyone. I nodded to them.

"That sounds great! When are we leaving?" I asked.

"As soon as my brother and a friend arrive," Damien answered.

"Your brother is coming here?"

He nodded.

"We'll fly to the castle. It's way faster than walking. But I can't fly everyone by myself. So, I asked Arius to come here along with Blake, one of our strongest warriors. They'll be able to fly with you while I fly with my sweet Kate in my arms."

Kate smiled at his last words and brushed a kiss on his lips.

That sounded great! I've only flown once so far, but it was awesome! And it was, indeed, faster than going on foot.

"Perfect! I'll get ready," I answered, pulling on Steven's hand.

Kate and Damien continued further. They wanted to talk with our mother about the baby before we departed for the vampire's castle. Well, I keep thinking the "vampire's castle," but I guess I should call it my sister's castle, now that she was the vampire Queen. I guess the name is stuck in my head. I laughed to myself.

As I walked with Steven to my room, I kept thinking about the fact that Elwin found a new book on demons. That was great news. I hoped it would contain more details that we could use against Eurynomos. And just as I was thinking those thoughts, I heard him in my mind.

"Hahaha! You fool! Keep dreaming, you'll never learn how to defeat me! Neither how to break the curse! You're just wasting your energy."

He was really getting on my nerves. As long as the curse was in place, he was able to know everything that was going on in my life, even up to my thoughts. If I managed to find a way to break the curse, it would mean he would know about it, too. I only hoped he wouldn't try to interfere.

Right on cue, I heard. *"You can count on it! You're never getting free of my curse!"*

I cursed out loud. I turned around as I heard someone's laugh behind me, to see my mate, Steven, laughing.

He embraced me and I let myself relax in his arms, feeling the warmth of his body, my heart beating strong.

"You think it's funny?"

He shook his head.

"Sorry my love, I couldn't help myself."

I couldn't be mad at him. He didn't hear the demon speak to me. He couldn't know to what extent it was annoying. I sighed.

"I know… It's just that… Having him speak to me all the time, trying to bring me down all the time. It's really hard on me. And as if it wasn't enough, I must endure hearing his thoughts as well. And let me tell you, the thoughts of a demon aren't really something you want to hear."

Steven tightened his embrace a little. His love lifted the weight of this curse a little, and made me feel slightly better.

"I know. I mean, I don't know. But I'm guessing it must be very hard and not really enjoyable."

"Yeah… You have no idea!"

I walked to our bed and prepared a small bag. I knew we would probably stay at my sister's castle for a few days. I loved going there. We had our own room now at the castle, so I didn't have to bring too much stuff. Steven was done a little after me.

We exited the pack's house and were greeted by Kate and Damien. Two other men were with them. The first one was very tall, with short white hair. I knew it was Arius, Damien's younger brother. He had already proved he could be trusted during the war that had happened two years earlier. He even helped Steven and me when we were overrun by vampires during that fight. But I didn't know the other vampire by their side. He looked younger. He was as tall as Damien. His muscles were showing through his shirt. He had black hair coming to his shoulders and tattoos all over one arm. He looked very strong.

Damien smiled as we approached.

"Bianca, Steven, you already know my brother Arius?"

"Yes," we both answered at the same time.

Arius came forward and hugged us. Like all vampires, he was slightly cold to the touch. His hug felt warm anyway.

Damien continued, "This is Blake, one of our stronger warriors."

Blake bowed slightly forward before answering, "at your service."

I thought he looked handsome. Steven looked at Blake, and then at me. I could feel jealousy from him, which made me smile. It was useless for him to be jealous. Steven was my mate. Nobody could ever replace him.

I squeezed his hand lovingly.

He turned to me and said, "You're flying with Arius. I'm flying with Blake."

I held back the giggles that wanted to come out.

"Of course, my love," I only answered while placing a kiss on his cheek.

Steven turned red as I told him through our linked minds, "You don't need to be jealous, you're my mate."

He answered through our minds, "I know… But I saw the way you looked at him."

I almost giggled out loud. "You silly! There will always be only one man in my life."

I immediately felt Steven relax at those words. I knew he couldn't help it. Wolves always get very protective and jealous of their mates, especially around other males. I knew it was like that, but I was not about to walk around with blinders to avoid seeing other men.

After checking that we were ready, Damien took my sister into his arms, Blake grabbed Steven and Arius held me in his arms. In no time, we were flying in the air. I really enjoyed the feeling of freedom it gave. Vampires sure were lucky to be able to do it all the time, as much as they wanted. I raised my eyes to see Arius looking at me. He held me tight, making sure I wouldn't fall.

"What?"

He smiled at my question. "You look like you're enjoying yourself quite a lot."

I nodded. "Yes, I am. I don't get to do this very often."

"Then buckle up, we'll make it worth the trip," he added before taking a turn to the right and plunging towards the ground. I grabbed him tight as I screamed while he laughed. He began doing all kinds of loops in the air. I felt like I was on a roller coaster. It was such a thrill! After a while, we were both laughing like kids.

When we finally arrived at the castle, everyone was already there.

Steven came running to me. "What were you guys doing?"

I looked at Arius, who was grinning as much as me. I laughed. "Just having a little fun!"

"Gosh, you guys had me worried! I thought something was wrong when I saw you guys go to the ground."

Arius replied, "Sorry for the scare. Don't worry, I'll always take good care of your mate."

Steven laughed a little. He looked embarrassed. Passing his hand through his hair, he answered, "I know. Sorry, I shouldn't have worried like that. I waited so much for her to wake up from that curse two years ago. My wolf still gets a little jumpy when she's not with me."

Arius gave a knowing smile. I heard from Kate that he once had found his mate, but his own father had brutally murdered her. He knew more than anyone what it felt like to lose his mate, or be scared for her well-being. Steven gave a manly tap on Arius's back, and we all got inside the castle.

As soon as we set foot inside the castle, Arius and Blake excused themselves. Kate and Damien had things to discuss as well. Being the Queen and the Lord of the vampires meant they had a lot of work and responsibilities. They rarely had a chance to take a break from it. They also took Eurynomos's threat very seriously. Ever since they learned that he was trying to open a gate to get into our world two years ago, they've been trying to rally every vampire city to our cause, preparing for a great war against the demon. I heard the preparations were going great, and a lot of warriors rallied for our cause. I've heard some warriors from distant countries decided to join as well… But I really hoped we didn't have to go to war with the demon and his army. I've seen the size of his army through my curse that binds me to him. If a war was to happen, a lot of people would die.

"You can count on it! I intend to murder every one of your friends. But you… I reserve a special treatment for you…" a sick laughter resonated through my head. I shivered at that thought. I didn't want to find out what this special treatment was.

I just hated that demon so much! "Won't you just shut up?" I screamed at him in my head.

Steven saw my face. "It's him again, isn't it?"

Although we were mates, and we could communicate through our minds, he couldn't hear what the demon said to me or my answers to the demon. I didn't quite understand why. It has been explained to me that it's like a communication link. Like when you dial a phone number on your phone. You reach the exact person you're trying to.

I've heard that through the ages, a few people have been able to speak to multiple people through their minds. As for me, I knew that a part of my soul was still trapped with Eurynomos in the Underworld. It explained the reason why I was bound to him and able to talk to him.

I nodded to Steven. He hugged me tight. I buried my nose in the crook of his neck, taking a deep breath of his sweet scent. He gently stroked my back with his hand. He always knew how to comfort me.

"Come, let's get our things into our room already," he whispered in my ear.

Steven and I knew the castle very well. It was a second home to us. We dropped our bags into our room and made our way to Elwin's laboratory.

Just as we were about to open the door, it opened itself, a strange smell exiting the room. Zach and Lilith came out of the room, holding hands.

I loved my uncle Zach. He didn't live with the pack since he had turned into a vampire. But I loved him the same as when he was only a werewolf. He kept the same color of skin as before, and you wouldn't even guess he was a vampire if it wasn't for his colder body temperature. They said the werewolf within him was strong enough that it fought with the vampire's virus and allowed him to keep the same skin color as before he turned into a vampire. I wondered if his wolf was different, now that he was a vampire.

"Hey! If it isn't Bianca and Steven!" Zach shouted happily before hugging us.

"Hi, Uncle Zach," I said happily. Then I turned to Lilith. She had braided her black ebony hair. Her hair always astounded me. It was going down to her knees, even braided. I thought maybe she was keeping them long in case she would need to use them to get a prince up her window. I giggled to myself at that thought.

Her skin was white as snow, as always. Even for a vampire, her skin was whiter than others. And her lips kept a blood-red tint that made them look almost unreal. She always was a beauty and looked happier than ever now that she was united with my uncle forever.

"Hi, Lilith, it's so nice to see you again," Steven told her.

She smiled at us before giving us a big hug.

"It's been a long time," she commented. It was true. It's been a while since we came to the castle.

"Too long," I agreed.

"So, are you ready to check on the war preparations?" Zach asked Steven.

He nodded to them.

Since I was bound to Eurynomos, and he could see everything I see, I wasn't able to help with the war preparations. Steven was allowed to help, as long as he said nothing to me. He found it hard to hide things from me, as he expressed to me already. But I reminded him that it was for a good reason, and so he agreed to do whatever he could to help with war preparations.

I took Steven's hand in mine, pulling him to me before he left. He grabbed my hips with his other hand, bringing me closer to him. I closed my eyes as our lips met. I could never have enough of his taste. I played with his short blond locks while we kissed. We broke the kiss, and I stared at his deep blue eyes.

"Have fun with your war preparations, my love. You'll know where to find me when you're done."

Steven squeezed my hand. "You can count on it. I love you to the moon and back."

I watched as Steven got away with Zach and Lilith. Already speaking lively about what was to come. I knew I could rely on them for the war preparations. Lilith was one of the best generals the vampires had.

"See, you have no chance, demon!" I told Eurynomos in my head before heading to Elwin's laboratory.

As I opened the door, the same strange smell hit me. It smelled a little like burned caramel. It was making me a little hungry. I would surely eat a burnt-caramel custard right now! But now was not the time to think about eating, I reminded myself.

Going into Elwin's laboratory, you would never know what to expect. The only thing you could know for sure is that it would be cluttered with all kinds of things, ranging from dead animals in liquid jars, skulls and vials, old books, and dust piling up on shelves. It seemed that everywhere you looked, you could find something you didn't see the last time you came into the room. There were all kinds of tools and contraptions that only Elwin knew what they were used for. Would I really want to know what they were for? I guess it was better I didn't. I chuckled to myself.

Elwin was bent over his experiment, not even noticing me. He was busy dissecting an animal with his sharp nails and pouring a strange liquid inside of it at the same time. Orange-colored fumes were rising from the animal's body. That's where the scent was coming from. I didn't want to interrupt, so I watched silently. When Elwin looked done with what he was doing, he took a step back to look at the result.

I took this as an opportunity to speak to him, as he still hadn't noticed me.

"What are you working on, Elwin?"

He startled at my question and turned to face me. He wasn't very tall, and his back was permanently curved from all the work he was doing. The gray started to show a lot in his hair, which meant he was very old, especially since vampires live for hundreds of years. I never dared asking his age, and I wondered if he even remembered himself.

He smiled when he realized I was there.

"Oh, my sweet Bianca! I am so happy to see you! Come! Take a look!"

He seemed very excited to show me his experiment. There was a dead animal's body in a small puddle of blood, with clumps of hair lying around it. The head was missing, so I couldn't know exactly what it was. The body was open and filled with a strange liquid. The fume seemed to emit from where the liquid touched the flesh.

I looked at Elwin with inquisitive eyes. He was waiting for a reaction of some sort from me. Then, realizing that I didn't understand what he was doing, he apologized.

"I'm so sorry! I should have explained first. You see, someone has freshly caught this rabbit this morning. I kept it alive up until the point I started this experiment. The poor thing didn't suffer, though. I always make sure to be gentle with living creatures."

I was relieved to hear that last part. Elwin knew how much I valued every life, whether human, vampire, werewolf, animal or even insects… well, okay, maybe not mosquitoes. He then continued with his explanations.

"You see, I'm looking for a way to locate the soul in the body." He was holding a vial in his hands. He continued, "the liquid in this vial is actually Psyche's tears."

My mouth fell open at that name.

"You mean THE Psyche? The soul goddess herself?" I exclaimed, interrupting him.

Elwin smiled at me.

"That very same goddess, my child. Those are very rare, but I got a hold of her tears in this vial. Don't ask me how I got them. I know a lot of people and pulled the right strings to get them. Suffice to say, it was hard to get a hold of them, but now, I'm on a quest to find the soul."

I stared in awe at his vial. I was speechless. God only knows where or how he got those tears. I was guessing they were surely hard to find and must be selling at a good price on the underground market. I preferred not to know all the details. And while this was all very interesting, this was not the reason I came to his lab. I had my own urgent matters to deal with.

"This all looks very fascinating, but you know why I'm here."

Elwin raised a finger in the air while exclaiming, "Right! I almost forgot!"

He turned around and went to one of his big wooden shelves decorating the walls. Lots of books were lined up on the shelf. A few of them looked very old and dusty. Some of them looked like they were bound in animal hide. Others were severely damaged. One of them had a part of his side missing, the pages barely holding together. I wondered what they were about. Elwin grabbed a few big leather books. These didn't have any dust on them. They looked like they were added recently to his collection.

"Here you go, my sweet child."

My eyes sparkled as I read the title of the first book, "Of Demons and The Underworld." I guessed that the other books were on similar subjects as well. I was impatient to start reading them.

"I found these at the back of the castle's library the other day. I'm sure the secrets they hold will help you against Eurynomos."

"Oh, thank you so much!" I almost screamed as I was so excited. I couldn't help myself but to jump a little bit.

Elwin grinned. He might be an old vampire sorcerer. He always seemed eager to help and happy when he proved useful.

"I've also worked on trying to find a cure for your father," he continued. He gestured me to follow him as he made his way to a stone bookstand in the back of the room. The foot of the bookstand was made of gray stone, carved with intrinsic patterns. It was a marvel to see.

On top was a big book, with a fabric bookmark inside, so you wouldn't lose the page it was open to. The light from the window shone on it, making the letters look like they were glowing.

I gazed at the book while waiting for Elwin to explain to me what this book was about.

"I've found this book describing elven herbs. For the most part, I already knew about them. But this one here," he said, pointing to the open page with his finger. "I had never heard of it."

I looked at the book. There was a drawing of a long stalk coming straight up with a few long leaves growing from the bottom of the plant. On top of it were hundreds of small white flowers completely covering the top of the stem. I read the name of it out loud, "Angelus Hyssopus."

"Yes," said Elwin. "The Angel Hyssop. I already about knew the Common Hyssop. It grows about everywhere on elven lands. Their flowers are purple, and it makes a very delicious tea. But I had never heard of the Angel Hyssop."

"Okay," I interrupted. "But what does it do?"

Elwin frowned a little. "Patience, my child! I was getting to that."

He composed himself again and then continued, "This plant is said to hold the highest healing powers. It is believed to protect against the plague and is used to purify sacred places. I believe we should try to retrieve it and prepare a concoction for your father."

This flower sounded wonderful! My heart was beating fast, and I couldn't hold my excitement.

"This is perfect! Where do we get this flower?"

"The Angel Hyssop is very rare. It is said to only grow at high altitudes, where there is water in abundance. Every attempt to make it grow indoors has failed. When cut, it must be immediately wrapped into a cloth and brought back as soon as possible, or the flower will wither too fast, and its magic properties will be lost."

"So, let me get this straight. We're not sure where it grows. We know it's rare, and it has to be brought back immediately, or else it won't work."

Elwin nodded. I shook my head a little. This will be more of a challenge than I thought. I had very little knowledge of the elven lands. And even if we found it, I wasn't sure it would work. *But* I knew it was worth trying. I didn't want Father to die. He's been in his bed, suffering, for more than two years now. I had to at least try.

"Okay, thanks Elwin. I will begin reading the books you gave me about the demons. And I will begin looking into the elven lands to see if I can find a place that could be growing the Angel Hyssop."

"At your service, my sweet lady," said Elwin, before going back to his previous experiments on the soul.

I left his laboratory and made my way to the castle's interior garden. I loved going to that garden! Very tall tree framed it with a few flower patches. There always seemed to have a lot of butterflies flying around those flowers. I sat on one of the benches. It was my favorite place to read.

It surprised me that Eurynomos had nothing to say about everything that had just happened. Was he scared? Maybe we were on to something? This gave me hope. I opened the first book, *"Of Demons and The Underworld,"* and began reading.

Chapter 3 (Will)

Fated mate

I was in the meeting hall of the pack's house, studying a map. I had already rallied all the neighboring packs to our cause. If Eurynomos was to succeed in his plan to travel to the world of the living, we would need all the help we could get. Now came a difficult choice. Should I go further, to seek the more distant packs? Or should I try to rally the rogue werewolves' pack up to the north?

My advisors have told me that it wasn't worth trying to gain the rogues to join us. They were rogues anyway and didn't abide by our rules. But I wasn't so sure about that. To the north, a little further on the west side of the St.Lawrence River, stood the only know rogue pack. Usually, rogue wolves don't do packs. They live alone, or in mated pairs, refusing to abide to any society. But these intrigued me. They had decided to form a pack together. They don't follow the common werewolves' laws, but they have their own laws. I wondered if they could be trusted.

I did some quick calculations. The rogue's pack was only a few hours away. If they won't rally to our cause, I'll lose less than a day. Worst case, if they try to attack me, I'm an Alpha. I should be more than capable of defending myself. However, if I was to decide to go see the wolf packs that lived further, I would need more than a week just to travel there, and then the same to come back. It seemed to me that going to the rogue's pack was a better choice. And if it didn't work, I could always prepare for a longer trip, anyway.

As I exited the meeting hall, I bumped into Marcus, one of the oldest advisors. His gray hairs were short, and he had a thick gray beard as well. Despite his age, he continued to do daily patrols of the pack's territory. He took the pack's security to heart, but I knew he also had his own personal reasons for patrolling. He was now too old to fight, but he was wise. I suspected he could still pack a punch, would someone trespass on the pack's territory. I respected him greatly. He was one of my father's best friends.

"My Alpha," he bowed to me.

"Marcus, please, no need to be so formal with me, old friend."

He got back up and smiled.

"I will always pay my respects to my Alpha."

"You already have. I will never doubt your loyalty."

Marcus smiled at my last words.

"Have you decided on your next destination?"

I nodded to him.

"Yes, I will be visiting the rogue wolves' pack."

Marcus jerked his head back, surprised. He fiddled with his fingers while answering, "But… You know rogue wolves can't be trusted, right? What makes you think they will listen to you?"

I shrugged my shoulders.

"I don't know, but they've been living in peace for years, not too far from our borders. I say it's worth the trip."

Marcus didn't seem completely convinced, but I didn't need him to be. I was the Alpha; I was making the decisions here.

"Whatever you wish," he simply answered.

I sighed; I didn't want to be rude to an old friend. I came closer to him, putting my hand on his shoulder.

"Listen, Marcus, I know you don't agree with me. But please understand my reasons. If this war happens, we will need all the wolves that we have. Even humans! This rogue's pack is less than a day away. They could prove useful if a war breaks."

Marcus let out a breath he was holding.

"Yes, you are right. I will let my own opinion on rogue wolves aside for the greater good of the pack."

I knew Marcus didn't like rogue wolves. One of his best friends was killed by one, years ago. His friend was just passing by in the woods and a rogue wasn't very far. For a reason still unknown, the rogue killed his friend. Marcus tried to run after this rogue wolf as fast as he could, but the rogue was able to escape. He got away and nobody ever saw him again. Only Marcus remembers his scent. He spent the rest of his life trying to see if he could find the scent of this wolf on our pack's territory, and still does today. I know it's the reason he continues to patrol the pack's borders.

"If you happen to smell the wolf's scent somewhere in that pack, we will refrain from associating ourselves with them. Would that please you?"

Marcus put his hand on his heart as he gasped. He seemed to relax a little and smiled.

"Yes, thank you! That would be great!"

Happy with his reaction, I turned around to go check on Jane. I wanted to see her before I went to take care of the rogues' pack.

Jane had been Luna for a few days now. I wanted to make sure she felt confident. I also wanted to make sure the pack respected her before I left. I found her in our room, looking at some documents, sitting at the desk. I still couldn't resign myself to mark her. I didn't know why, but my wolf didn't seem eager to do it.

Still right now, sitting in the chair reading, she was beautiful, and my heart fluttered at her sight. She was a wonderful she-wolf, and I loved to kiss her and please her until she screamed my name. I really didn't understand what was holding back my wolf. I tried to speak to him. I knew he was really hoping to find our fated mate. But I clearly told him that Jane was our mate now. He hasn't spoken to me since then. He shut himself up completely, and it felt strange to lose that connection with my wolf. I guessed it was only a matter of time before he accepted her, and everything went back to normal.

I walked into the room. Jane raised her head from the document she was reading and smiled at me as I walked towards her. She rose, her emerald eyes staring at my soul. I pulled her to me, wrapping my arm around her waist. She raised herself on her tippy toes, bringing her delicious lips to mine. Our tongues twirled together. I could feel my heart beating strong and my breath quickening. I groaned a little when she broke the kiss.

"Oh Jane, you taste like paradise. I could spend my whole day in your arms."

She giggled a little.

"Too bad you have Alpha tasks to do," she teased.

I almost forgot what I needed to talk about…

"That reminds me, I will need to leave for a day."

"Why?" she asked, clearly not happy about this.

I sighed. "Alpha stuff… I need to go see the rogues' pack to the north."

Jane crossed her arms over her chest.

"Can't you send someone else? You barely spend time with me. I understand you have your duties, but I wish you'd stay with me."

I grabbed her hands, gently squeezing them.

"Jane, I wish I could. But this is an important matter. I wouldn't want this to fail because I didn't go by myself."

Jane got closer and leaned on my chest. Her warm breath was blowing softly on my neck.

"I understand. I just wanted to spend more time with you. And you know… maybe our wolves would get to know each other more."

I knew she was impatient for my wolf to accept her as our mate. I knew she wanted to be marked. Spending more time together would surely help speed up the process.

"What if I only left tomorrow? We could spend the rest of the day together."

Jane had the biggest smile.

"Really? You would do that for me?"

"Of course!" I smiled back.

She put her hands around my neck and kissed me once again, nibbling on my lower lips. I could smell the scent of her arousal. How I wished to take her right now.

I began bringing her towards the bed while kissing. Her breathing was quickening, and her hands started to roam my body. I could already feel the bulge in my pants growing.

Just as I was about to remove Jane's shirt, the door to our room opened, slamming into the wall.

"Who the heck enters my room without knocking?" I snarled, angry.

A lookout stood there, out of breath. His eyes opened wide, he made a movement back.

"I… I'm sorry, my Alpha…" he stuttered while fidgeting with his fingers. "A rogue wolf has been seen in our territory."

My anger suddenly fell.

"Where?"

"To the north of the territory, near the border."

"Thank you, I will go now!"

The lookout seemed relieved. I turned to Jane, who had a knowing look on her face. Our time together just had been shortened again.

"Sorry," I told her.

She shook her head. "It's okay. You're the Alpha. Go!"

I ran outside the house. I didn't even take the time to remove my clothes before letting my wolf take control of me. He was practically slamming through my head, asking to let him out. My clothes got torn apart, but I didn't care. Running in my wolf form would be way faster than going on foot.

I ran as fast as I could, letting my senses guide me. When I started to get closer to the border of the territory, I caught the faint scent of a wolf. I didn't know what it was, but it smelled… so good. I tried to remind my wolf we needed to go after the rogue wolf that was seen in our territory, but he didn't care anymore. All he wanted to do was to follow the scent.

The closer we got, the stronger the scent got. I have to admit; it did smell good, and I was dying to know who smelled like that. It was an undeniable pull. It was so strong, I couldn't resist; I didn't want to resist.

I followed the scent. It was now so strong; I could make the sweet scent of jasmine and citrus. That scent was just driving me crazy! Finally, I found where the scent was coming from. A woman was standing not too far in front of me. She had beautiful tawny skin. She had numerous tattoos on her arm and three pairs of earrings. Her hair was long, black, and curly. Tight leggings were hugging her legs, the sight of them lighting a fire inside of me. Her shirt revealed her shoulders before flowing loosely. She was armed with a bow.

I looked at her aura and saw that it was pure and strong. I thought she was simply the most beautiful woman I had ever seen. She looked like a raw gemstone to me. And she was a shifter, too. I could feel her wolf. My wolf was screaming inside my head, "mate! Claim! She's ours!" But… but it couldn't be true. I already had a Luna. I couldn't leave Jane, just like that. Not after introducing her to the pack and working so hard to get everyone to trust her.

Surely, the woman must have been feeling the bond pull, too. She was staring at me intensely. She wasn't scared of my wolf one bit, even if I was an Alpha and my wolf was huge. There was no use trying to hide myself. I changed back to my human form so I could speak with her. I could read hunger in her eyes, staring at my naked body. However, she turned her head a little and got a pair of jeans out of her bag, throwing them at me. The jeans had her scent all over them from being in her bag. I had to refrain myself from burying my nose in them to have a good scent of her smell. I wondered what was she doing with a man's pair of pants in her bag? Did they belong to a special someone? A low growl escaped my chest at that thought.

She smirked at that sound, as if reading my mind.

"I always keep all kinds of clothes with me. You never know when you might need them," she explained. Of course, she couldn't know what I was thinking, since I didn't mark her, and we had just met. I guess it was just obvious.

"Who are you?" I asked. "What are you doing in my pack's territory?"

"I'm Leila, from the Hands of Fate pack."

Leila, what a beautiful name, I thought. It sounded so feminine. Yet, at the same time, her name held a force to it. A little bit like her, she was both strong and beautiful at the same time. I shook my head. What was I thinking? Gosh Will, concentrate! I thought to myself.

"I have never heard of your pack before."

She put a hand on her hip while thinking, making her curves even more tempting.

"Oh yeah! You might call us by the name of rogue wolves, or something like that."

Did she just say, "rogues"? She would be the rogue my lookout spotted on our territory. That can't be! There's no way an Alpha can be mated to a rogue! This was not good, not good at all. My wolf disagreed. He didn't care she was a rogue. But I reminded him, we already have a mate waiting for us. He growled at me, but I didn't care. I had my responsibilities as the Alpha of the pack.

"You didn't answer my question. What are you doing in my pack's territory?"

Leila looked at me with her deep chocolate brown eyes. I could feel the mate bond pulling me strongly. All I wanted to do was to give in. I knew she felt it, too.

"A few days ago, I caught a glimpse of your scent. I had to find where it was coming from. And now I do," she added with a smile. That smile of hers melted my heart. How I wish that I could make her mine.

But I couldn't. I already had a Luna. The pack accepted Jane as their Luna; I couldn't just replace her like that. And there was no way the pack would accept a rogue Luna.

"I already have a mate." I spoke as coldly as I could, trying to hide my emotions.

Leila took a step back as I said those words. She put a hand on her mouth as she said in a shaky voice, "that can't be."

My heart was tearing apart inside, and my wolf was furious against me. I knew I was hurting her, and it was hurting me to do so. But I knew this was the right choice to do, as the Alpha of the pack. I had responsibilities, and they came first. I cleared my throat.

"It is, although she is not my fated mate. But I do have a mate."

I tried to hide my feelings as much as I could, but I knew she probably could feel at least part of it since we were fated mates.

"Then reject me! That way, it will be done, and we will be free from this bond." She was furious now. I could see the pain in her eyes, and I was so sorry for causing it. I could also see how strong she was. How I wish I could get to know her fully. My wolf kept screaming at me, "mate! Claim her! We need her!" But I kept ignoring him.

"I, Will, of the pack of the Southern Forest, reject…"

All of my life I had been looking for my fated mate. Today, I finally found her. What was I doing? Should I really reject her? What about my responsibilities as Alpha? What about Jane? If I rejected her, the mate bond would be broken. It would hurt for a while, but she would get over it and so would I. But if I did that, I would lose the chance the Moon Goddess has given me to find the one made for me. Should I really do that?

My head was full of doubts. I didn't know what to do anymore. I wanted to sit down; I couldn't think straight anymore.

I looked at Leila, who had her eyes closed, like she was bracing for the impact of the mate bond severing. Did I really want to put her through that pain? Even with her eyes closed, she looked perfect. Her lips looked tantalizing; I had to refrain from giving in and kissing her.

Realizing I wasn't speaking anymore, she opened her eyes.

"Well? Get on with it already! This is already as painful as it is!" Her voice was shaky.

I felt sick. I couldn't answer anything, a knot forming in my throat. I wished I could comfort her. She sighed.

"Fine! Then I'll do it! I, Leila, of the Hands of Fate pack, rej…"

I didn't let her time to finish. I shouted, "No you don't!"

She looked surprised and before she could try to finish her sentence, I turned back into my wolf shape; tearing up the pants she had given me, and ran as fast as I could to the pack's house. I knew she wouldn't follow me.

My mouth fell open. I couldn't move, as I watched, stunned, my mate running away. What the hell just happened? He was the one saying he had a mate. Why didn't he let me reject him? At least we could have been freed from this cursed bond. What good was there to find your fated mate when he doesn't want you? Now, my wolf will never be satisfied as long as I don't find him again. Did he want to keep this power over me and his other mate as well? What a presumptuous guy! Why would the Moon Goddess mate me with someone like that? Fate is so hard to understand!

I looked to the ground where he was standing just a few seconds before. Those jeans I had given him, all ripped apart. It was one of my best pairs. As I approached from the pieces on the ground, I couldn't help myself. I picked one of the pieces and brought it to my nose. Taking a deep breath, I realized it smelled like him. My wolf was immediately overjoyed. She kept saying "mate" in my head. I tried to tell her he wanted to reject us, but she replied that he didn't… Which was true. I guess I'll have to find him another day to finish this. As much as I didn't want to, I took the piece of jeans with me, folding it neatly into my bag. I picked up my bow and started walking back to my pack's territory.

Well, today sure ended up being a lousy day. Here I was, hoping to find my mate and find love. But instead, I find an arrogant male that prefers his other mate than me. I mean come on! The one chosen by the Moon Goddess! I can't believe the nerves he has! I can't believe his wolf accepts this! My wolf would never agree to settle for someone other than her fated mate. An occasional date maybe, but not permanently. If I was in a couple with a man and found my fated mate, I would go with my fated mate immediately! Any wolf would understand that! Finding your fated mate was a blessing. There was only one person made especially for you. You don't say no to the Moon Goddess.

I couldn't wait to tell Skye what had happened. At least she'll be there for me. I'm lucky to have such a good friend. That thought somewhat raised my spirits a little bit.

Chapter 4 (Leila)

Hands of Fate

The walk back to the pack helped clear my mind a little. My heart still wasn't settled, and my wolf kept asking me to go find him. But I was feeling a little better. Soon, I arrived in our little town. Well, I say town, but it's only a few rows of houses, really. We don't have any shops or schools. We go to the human cities for that, blending in with humans as our ancestors have always done, living in peace. Of course, we preferred to stay here in our little piece of heaven as much as possible.

Our pack was an ancient one. We have learned to live together, one with nature. We tried not to disturb the forest as much as possible. We built our houses only from the fallen trees, mixing the wood with stones, mud and leaves as necessary. We usually let plants grow on the sides and on the roofs of the houses. It absorbed the heat from the sun during summer, keeping the houses cool. Due to the plants growing on our houses, it also made them harder to detect to the untrained eye. We didn't want to attract any unnecessary attention.

It was a beautiful place to live in. Soon, I arrived at the main house in the town. This building was larger than the others. That's where I lived with my grandmother Ravynne. At sixty-two, she was the eldest of us. As it might not be very old, I was told that a few years before I was born, there was a sudden attack from orcs on the town. Nobody ever knew where they came from, or why they decided to attack us. All that I know is that all the adults of the pack went and fought, protecting the young ones. Our pack was strong, but despite the wolves and the magic powers that we held, almost everyone was killed. That day, my grandmother suddenly became the oldest member of the pack and the chieftess.

We didn't abide to the Alpha's society order like other wolf packs. I think that's one of the reasons we were called rogue wolves. Our society was matriarchal, which goes against every other wolf pack that I've encountered so far. In our pack, we valued the wisdom of the oldest members. It was also the oldest members that taught the young ones everything they couldn't learn in the human schools, like magic. We didn't only have werewolves in our pack, but also of witches. Some of us, like myself, were werewolf witches. Born as a wolf, but also with magic powers. My grandmother, as well as a few older pack members, remembered the ancient secrets of the witches' magic powers.

As I approached my house, I saw my grandmother sitting on the porch, telling a story to the children. They were hanging on her lips as she told, once more, the story of the night of the orc attack. We made sure to tell the stories of our pack, from generation to generation, making sure they were never forgotten.

I sat with the kids, listening to the rest of the story, waiting for my grandmother to be finished. I watched as kids opened their mouths wide as she told her story. Some kids, shutting their eyes or looking through their fingers when they got scared. One of them even gasped and blocked her ears with her hands. It was so cute to see the admiration of the children. I could see the story unfold in their little minds.

When my grandmother was done telling the story, she got up. I came to hug her. She was so pretty, with her white long hair coming down her lower back. A few braids here and there complimented her look.

She was wearing her usual black bear skin cape over a simple cotton dress that flowed to her ankles. She wore a leather belt made from deer hide. A few trinkets hung from her belt, as well as a satchel. She always kept basic herbs in it, in case she needed to brew an emergency remedy or poison. My grandmother was not a werewolf. She was a witch. She couldn't transform into her animal when in danger. But her magic was very powerful. She knew how to cure people and how to hurt her enemies.

My grandmother was the only family I had left. I loved her very dearly. She had raised me when my parents were brutally murdered by some humans. My dad was working in the human city nearby and got friendly with some humans. He thought he could trust them. At one point, he told them about being a werewolf. The next week, his friends invited my parents to eat with them. But they poured poison in my parents' meals, weakening them. Then they attacked my parents.

Because of the poison, they couldn't transform into their wolf form to defend themselves or use their magic. Whatever poison they had used; it must have been a strong one. My parent's corpses were found outside the human city by one of our lookouts. They had been missing for days. I tried not to think back to these memories. I was only a child, but it still hurt, even today.

"How was the search for your mate?" my grandmother inquired.

A lump formed in my throat; I felt my stomach tighten. I really didn't want to talk about it.

"Hey, why don't we talk about the planning of the next hunt?" I suggested. I was already feeling my voice beginning to shake. Just thinking of Will made me hurt.

My grandmother had a pained look on her face and reached out for me. I ran into her hug, letting the tears flow. I needed her comfort so badly; I didn't even realize it.

"Oh honey, it didn't go well, didn't it? Won't you tell me what happened?"

I sniffled. Being in my grandmother's arms was warming up my heart a little, and I felt a little better.

"What the hell did he do to my best friend?" asked a voice behind me.

I turned my head to see Skye.

I've known Skye for as long as I could remember. We've always been friends. She was small, had black straight hair coming to her shoulders and liked to wear sophisticated dresses she bought in human towns. Skye wasn't born with an animal, contrary to me. She wasn't born with powers of the witches either. I loved her all the same. My grandmother always said that your powers, or lack of, don't define who you are. I knew she was right.

Being with my best friend and my grandmother, I felt better already.

"Skye! How nice of you to join us," my grandmother commented.

"Ravynne, it's always a pleasure to see you," Skye answered, smiling.

"Leila, my treasure. Care to tell us what happened when you found your mate?" my grandmother asked me.

I sighed. I owed them at least an explanation, even if I didn't feel like talking about it. I thought of the quickest and less painful way to tell them.

"He said he already has a mate." I figured that maybe I wouldn't have to talk further about it by saying that.

"What? I thought that was impossible!" exclaimed Skye.

I realized Skye thought that Will had another fated mate. That's not exactly how I meant it, I thought to myself. I didn't feel like talking about it either. I looked at my grandmother. She was looking at me with kind eyes. My grandmother knew me well enough. She understood without me saying anything.

"That's okay, Skye," she started. "We don't know everything the Moon Goddess has in store for us."

"But..." Skye wanted to protest.

"Now is not the time," my grandmother interrupted. "Come, it is time we prepare the plants for the witchcraft class on remedies."

Skye snorted and pinched her lips together. Then she sighed. "Fine, it's not like I have a choice in the matter," she complained.

My grandmother laughed a little, used to Skye's tantrums.

"Come now, Skye. You always have a choice in life," my grandmother answered.

I watched the two of them walking towards the house. I was happy that we didn't have to talk about my mate anymore. I knew Grandmother had to prepare the things for the witchcraft class. I also knew she didn't have to do it right away, and she was doing that for me, to get Skye to stop asking questions. I really felt grateful for that.

I went to pick up some leaves and plants I knew we would need for the witchcraft class. It would get my mind off from Will; at least I hoped. I loved to attend my grandmother's classes. Even though my witchcraft skills were well advanced, I loved to assist in any way that I can. I loved to help the little ones who struggled to succeed. Absently, I took the piece of jeans out of my bag and brought it to my nose. I couldn't help myself but to smile at his scent. This mate bond was sure messing with me. I quickly put it back into my bag before anyone saw me and went on to do my tasks.

The sun was already lowering on the horizon, setting the sky to blaze as it set. It was time for my grandmother's witchcraft class. I set aside the partridges I had hunted with my bow during the afternoon. I was one of the best archers in the pack.

Combined with my magic powers and my wolf, you could say I was well prepared for any situation.

Wood stumps and rocks formed a circle in the little valley next to our village. The children were already sitting on them, eager for the class to start. They were talking together, some of them bragging about how strong their magic was. It was funny to watch them, and to listen to their stories.

"I swear to you! I was able to do flames up this high!" said a little boy, raising his hand way above his head.

"That's impossible!" retorted a little girl.

"I swear to you," he answered back.

"I heard that Melissa got some flames twice as high as those," another girl whispered to them. They all gasped in admiration, imagining flames almost as high as the trees.

I had to refrain myself from giggling. I loved to see how carefree the children were. I was happy that our pack provided the protection for them to grow happily.

I took a deep breath, a spark of magic passing through my body, making me shiver. This was my favorite place to do witchcraft. The magic was strong within these lands. I could feel it flowing through my veins. On full moon nights, you could even see sparks of magic appearing here and there, when magic was at its fullest. Everyone loved my grandmother's classes. Even curious fairies had gathered and waited for her to begin. I loved to see their glow through the grass blades in the darkness of the forest.

At the center of the circle, was an area with moss and small plants. It was the perfect place to practice witchcraft, as everyone would have a good view.

My grandmother arrived, followed by Skye, who was holding a big basket full of prepared plants.

"Watch your steps now," my grandmother warned her.

Skye sighed at her comment. I knew Skye hated being told to be careful. But my grandmother was right, Skye tended to be clumsy. It wouldn't be great to stumble, while holding a basket full of reagents, in front of everyone. I knew my grandmother only said that for Skye, as she would probably be embarrassed if she was to trip.

When they arrived at the center of the circle, my grandmother signaled for me to come closer. We always started the witchcraft classes doing our pack's ancestor's sacred dance. Skye couldn't perform it since she wasn't born with magic powers. She took place behind the children, watching us. I always had the feeling she was feeling envious of me. I kept trying to push those thoughts away; Skye was my best friend; she was a sister to me. Yet every time I performed the dance with my grandmother, the same feeling crept over me.

I stood in front of my grandmother. We both closed our eyes and joined our hands, calling forth a small blue orb of magic in the air in front of us. My feet and hands began moving by themselves. I knew this dance so well; I didn't even have to think about it. With each turn of our feet and hands appeared another orb of magic. Each orb of a different color, depending on the element that had answered our call. Turn by turn, the earth, air, water, and fire came to us, lending us their power. With each movement of my hips, the orbs danced around us. It was a beauty in all, and the kids were in awe. We always finished this dance by signaling for the orbs to merge all together. Together, they merged into this one huge orb of white energy. It was so strong; it couldn't be contained. It flew to the sky and exploded, leaving multiple colored trace in the sky, just as fireworks would. All the kids were ecstatic in front of such beauty. In the back, Skye was pursing her lips while waiting for us to be finished.

The lights faded. At last, the witchcraft class could begin. I sat with the children while my grandmother started talking. Skye came by my side and sat with me.

"Nice job, as always," she whispered to me, smiling.

"Thanks," I whispered back.

We turned our attention to the class, keeping our attention on my grandmother, in case she needed our help with the class.

I ran back to the pack's house as fast as I could. My heart was hammering in my chest. My wolf was furious against me. My eyes were clouded, but I knew the path and didn't need to see straight. When I arrived in front of the pack's house, I transformed back into my human form. I shook my head, grabbing my face with my hands. My heart was beating fast, even though I wasn't running anymore. My heart hurt and I felt numb. What the hell just happened? Why couldn't I reject her? When she started saying the words, I couldn't bear to stay and listen to her. I couldn't let her do it. My wolf took control over me. He wouldn't accept rejection. It was clear to me he would never accept Jane as his mate. Not now that we've met our fated mate. That was for sure.

She was from the rogue's pack. I needed to cancel my trip. There was no way I was going to seek their help with the war. Marcus would be happy; I would go see the packs that lived further. I couldn't afford to see her again. It was painful enough as it is. If I saw her again, I didn't know if I could resist her. I had never felt a pull this strong before. It was like I was addicted to her, without ever having tasted her. If the fated mate bond was this strong, I could understand why they say this bond lasts forever. I took a few seconds to try to pull myself together again. I couldn't afford to look shaken off in front of the pack. I was the Alpha. I had to be strong. Keep it together, don't show your feelings. I took a deep breath before entering the pack's house.

I took a change of clothes in the entrance hall of the pack's house and got dressed. Putting my jeans on, I couldn't help myself but to think of the pair Leila had given me that I tore apart by changing into my wolf form. I felt bad, and I hoped she understood. I guess it didn't matter anymore, since I would never see her again. Somehow, that thought hurt way deeper than I thought it would.

Jane and the advisors came to see me when they heard I was in the pack house again. They were watching me, waiting to have my report on the situation. I looked at them. I was surrounded by people, yet I felt lonely.

"The rogue has been dealt with," I stated simply.

"Is he dead?" Marcus asked.

I shook my head. "This rogue meant no harm. She went back to her pack's territory."

I tried to keep a stern face, trying to hide my emotions. Inside of me, I was a total mess. I only hoped I managed to fool everyone.

"Thank you, my love," Jane spoke.

I looked at her. She was as beautiful as ever. But something felt broken in my heart. I knew it was my responsibility as the Alpha to keep her as Luna of the pack. As much as my wolf disagreed. There was no way I could have a rogue wolf as a mate. I felt grateful that Jane couldn't hear my thoughts. I didn't want to hurt her. This would be my pain, something I had to bear alone, as the Alpha. I hoped Jane could live happily with me, without knowing about it.

I knew I would suffer for a while, but it should lessen with time. I had all the time I needed to make things work with Jane. I hugged her. She rested her head on my chest. Inside, I felt hollow. I couldn't feel anything for her anymore. I didn't say anything, I couldn't find the words.

Marcus asked, "was she from the pack to the north?"

I nodded. Speaking about it made my heart ache. I swallowed hard.

"I will not go see the rogues' pack," I told them with authority.

"As you wish," Marcus answered. He seemed relieved by my decision.

"I need a few days. I will prepare to go see the Nunangat pack, up to the north," I added.

Marcus's eyes widened.

"The Nunangat pack? But that's way up north! Even going by plane, it would take about eight hours! And planes don't even go up to their pack. Besides, you're never going to be able to book a flight… The planes leave only once every few weeks for Nunangat."

"I know," I answered, "that's why I'm going to go by car."

"By car?" Marcus was stupefied. "But it's going to take you at least a week, and I'm not even sure there are roads all the way up there."

"That's why I'm going to take a few days to pack some things up, and to spend time with my Luna," I answered. Jane smiled at my last sentence.

My mind was set. Going this far to the north. That's what I needed to stop me from thinking about Leila. With that much distance between us, it should be easier.

Everyone nodded. I went off to begin preparing what I needed for the trip.

A few days later, I was almost ready to go to the Nunangat pack. I was eager to leave. The past few days didn't go well. I was a mess! I tried as much as I could to stop thinking about Leila, but I couldn't. My wolf ached from not seeing his fated mate. Every time I looked at Jane, I compared her to Leila. I was grumpy and numb. I felt like I had a hangover without even having drunk. I couldn't mark Jane, and even worse, I didn't even make love to her. Kissing her had become difficult, and I tried to avoid it as much as I could.

She knew something was wrong and asked me what it was numerous times, but I couldn't tell her. I barely ate anything, but I didn't feel hungry either. I tried to convince myself that it was for the greater good of the pack. My wolf was longing for Leila so much, he was restless. He couldn't care less about Alpha responsibilities.

Jane got me out of my thoughts.

"Will, you'll be leaving in two days. Will you at least spend a little bit of time with me before leaving?"

She looked sad. I knew I had neglected her in the past days. I shut myself down, got my walls up and didn't let anyone enter. It was only legitimate that I at least try to spend time with her before leaving.

"Yes, I'm sorry Jane. I know I haven't been the best mate lately." Just saying the word *mate* made me think of Leila. I pushed the pain to the back of my mind, trying to ignore it. Jane was right, I was leaving soon. I should try to spend the rest of the time I have here with her.

"Why don't we listen to a movie, like we used to do when we were younger?"

I smiled at Jane's suggestion. I used to love watching movies with her. I would always get closer to her while we watched the movie, little by little, without her noticing it. It was the perfect flirting move. I had perfected it so much over the years that I could be practically holding her in my arms by the end of the movie. Of course, now that Jane was my mate, I didn't need to hide myself. I could just cuddle with her right from the beginning of the movie.

"That's a great idea!" I answered.

Jane chose one of her favorite movies. It was a vampire romance movie. I didn't mind them; they usually had some action as well. We sat on the couch and Jane cuddled with me. Listening to the movie, with Jane's body close to me, I started to relax, and I felt my mind go free for the first time in days. It felt good, a break from the storm that was raging in my soul. I started to smell her skin, letting my lips graze gently on her neck, leaving soft kisses on their path. She turned to me and straddled on me.

We started kissing, our tongues dancing together. My heart was beating fast as I grabbed her hips with my hands. She started rocking her hips, fully clothed. I could feel my pants tightening up. How I wanted her right now! My eyes were closed from our kissing, but I could see it clearly in my mind. How her curly black hair was moving with each of her swings. I could picture her without even looking, her beautiful tawny skin, her tattoos. I was getting so aroused by now; I started taking down her clothes.

"Hmm… Will, you're so hot tonight," she commented while panting.

At that moment, when I heard Jane's voice, I realized that it wasn't Leila. I mean, how could I have mistaken them? They were so different one from another. What really hit me is how I yearned to kiss Leila… but not Jane. Who was I fooling?

I stopped dead and Jane was fixating me.

"Is something wrong, Will?"

What was I supposed to answer? That I was thinking of another woman? Of my true mate? And that it was hurting me inside out not to be with her? She would be devastated.

"I'm sorry… I can't," was all that I could manage to get out.

I stormed out of the room while Jane called for me, "Will, wait!"

It was already too late. I was already out of the room. I quickly removed my clothes and got outside. I changed as soon as I exited the pack's house.

The moon was already high in the sky. The stars were shining like diamonds. I needed to get away from here. I was lost and didn't know what to do anymore. My walls were destroyed. That shell I had built around myself was cracked. Everything I believed in, being the Alpha, my responsibilities, even my own heart. Everything crumbling to the ground, undone by a single encounter. How could I ever live like that? How I wish my father was able to help me through this. I needed his guidance so badly. Surely, he would have advice, wisdom gained from years of experience. I was feeling distraught, and it was tearing me apart inside. I ran as fast as I could, not thinking about anything. I let my wolf lead the way, letting him control me. I didn't even watch where we were going. I trusted him. I felt free, forgetting my duties, my pain. I really needed this.

After a while, I started to smell a scent. I couldn't forget this sweet scent of jasmine and citrus. It was her! How I longed to see her. I followed her scent, my wolf screaming in my head "mate," as we followed it. I ran as fast as I could, afraid to lose her scent, afraid that she would leave if I didn't go fast enough. She was the lifeboat I've been searching for, the last few days, in a storm where I was drowning.

I soon arrived at the limit of my pack's territory, to the north, pretty much at the same place where I had seen her the first time. However, there was no woman this time. I saw this beautiful black wolf staring at me. Her eyes were golden. Her stare held such fierce and passion. I approached gently, not wanting to scare her. Her wolf was completely black, except for a spot on the back of her neck that was golden, in the shape of a diamond. She was truly magnificent!

I saw her eyes flicker, and I knew her wolf wanted to meet mine. My wolf was more than happy to meet with her. All I could hear in my mind was "mate." And since we were both in our wolf form already, it would be a piece of cake to let them meet. I gave all the space my wolf needed, going back in my mind as much as I could. I approached her and proceeded to smell her. I was immediately overwhelmed by her enticing scent of jasmine and citrus. She proceeded to smell me too and rubbed her muzzle against mine. My wolf was swollen with pride at having his mate rubbing her scent on him. All the pain and sadness I have felt in the past few days were gone. I was feeling elated. My heart was racing. She seemed to be enjoying herself too. I could feel through our mate bond that she missed me as much as I missed her.

She was watching me, studying me, when suddenly, she started running. I laughed to myself, and a low rumble emanated from my chest. You want to play catch, my mate? Gladly, I thought to myself, smiling. I followed her through the forest, letting her take a little advance, then gaining on her. Even if I didn't see her, I could follow her scent easily. She wasn't trying to hide it; she wanted me to follow. I knew her wolf wanted mine. My wolf was more than willing to play her game. I would do anything to please her right now! After running for a while through the woods with her, I finally decided to catch up with her. She was very fast and nimble, but as an Alpha, I was faster than her.

When I finally caught up with her, I placed myself on top of her and held her head steady. My wolf spoke through my mind, up to hers, "mine." It was possessive and strong. Without even thinking, my wolf's teeth began to grow more, preparing to mark her, to make her mine forever. My heart was hammering in my chest. I wanted this as much as my wolf. Who cared about the wolf pack and my responsibilities? She was my mate, I needed her by my side. My pack will just have to accept her. There was no way I was losing her another time. As I prepared to bite her, I heard her voice in my head, "please don't."

I froze at those words. My human mind regaining a little bit of control over my wolf. What was I doing? Yes, she was my mate. Yes, I wanted her by my side. But I wanted her to agree with this. I didn't want to impose it on her. I released my hold on her. She looked at me with her beautiful almond eyes. She was the prettiest wolf I had ever seen in my whole life. I could feel through our bond that she was grateful I didn't mark her. I wondered how it was possible for me to hear her through my mind, even though the mating process was not done. Could it be possible for the mate bond to be this strong?

I wondered if I should turn back to my human body so that we could speak together. I only just had time to think about it, that she turned her back and began running in her pack's direction. I looked around me, I wasn't even in my pack's territory anymore. I started walking back, thinking about what had just happened. I couldn't believe that my wolf was ready to mark her, to make her ours, right here, right now. Her sweet scent was still lingering in my nose. I couldn't stop thinking about Leila. She was so precious; she was like a treasure to me.

I made my way back to the pack's house and changed back to my human form. Everyone was asleep already, as the night was well advanced. I entered my room without making a noise. Jane was asleep. She had dried tears on her face, and I immediately felt bad. I knew she loved me, and I knew she wanted pups. I was the one dragging her into this. I was the one who asked her to be my Luna. She accepted all the responsibilities that came with it, all for me. Would I be able to give her what she needed? Should I just give up already? I was feeling tired and confused by everything that had happened. Taking care not to wake her up, I lay down by her side and put an arm on her hips. I tried to concentrate on Jane only, trying to remember the reasons I loved her, while slowly falling to slumber.

Chapter 5 (Eurynomos)

The breach

This was taking longer than I had anticipated. I was getting rather impatient! Couldn't those incompetent fools work any faster? I watched as a group of goblin wizards were slowly wearing down the spell that sealed the portal. They wore a long brown-greenish tunic with a hood. It seemed like their tunic had been sewn from multiple pieces of fabric and they didn't exactly match in color. Holes were made through the hood of their tunic so that their ears may go through. Their red eyes seemed to glow with the reflection given by the flowing lava. It contrasted against their yellowish-gray skin. They were casting a spell in their native language. I couldn't understand what they were saying, but I couldn't *care less. They knew they would face my wrath if they were to fail. They knew better than to face the anger of the Underworld's ruler.*

Suddenly, a loud cracking sound came from the portal, followed by a deep rumble. The lava that seemed to flow evenly on its surface before, was now forming balls and lumps and was uneven. One of the goblin wizards came towards me. He wasn't very tall and carried a wooden staff mounted with the razor-sharp claw of some big creature. He wore a long cape on his back and had a pair of shoes made of animal hide. He bowed lowly in front of me and smiled, showing his sharp, hooked teeth. He spoke with a high-pitched guttural voice, in a broken English.

"Master, it has begun."

"What has begun?"

"A breach."

I laughed so loudly, the sound of my laughter echoing against the rock faces. Every creature in Tartarus stopped what they were doing and trembled in terror. They would do well to fear me, for soon, I shall reign over both the dead and the living.

I turned to the goblin wizard in front of me. He had an unsure look on his face, clutching his hands together, his long sharp nails digging into his own skin.

"Perfect!"

The goblin seemed to relax a little bit.

"Tell the others to start casting the exit portals spell. We need all the exits we can get for my army to cross to the world of the living."

"But… but master. We… we'll need to stop working on the portal," he stuttered while looking at the ground.

"You shall keep working on the portal while the others work on the exits," I snarled.

"Yes… yes, right away," he whimpered away.

I laughed at the thought I could easily crush them all with my force. The idea was tempting, but they were still useful to me. Maybe when their task would be done, I would pick a few goblins to kill for fun. Now that would be entertainment.

Now that the portal was breached, my army could start going to the mortal world. I was still bound to the underworld, while the seal was not completely broken. But at least we could cast secondary exit portals. It didn't allow as many people to get through at a time, but it wouldn't be long before we would breach the main portal. Then, I'll be unstoppable!

The best part was that by casting multiple exits, I will be able to start invading the world at multiple spots at the same time. This was perfect! And still, there was only one entry into the underworld. I would make sure it was heavily guarded... only a fool would try to get in anyway.

When the main portal's seal will be broken, I'll be able to travel to the world of the living myself. With all the living energy I'm draining from mortal creatures, I'm getting stronger and stronger by the minute. You hear that? You wretched wench! You will never stop me! I couldn't help myself from laughing, as I knew very well the girl could hear everything I told her. I loved to torment her. She will never be free from me. There was no way they could manage to free her. I rejoiced myself. Not only were things going great, but I also knew that the wench was drowning in despair at my success.

I was sitting at my desk, checking a few documents. We had a few thousand warriors joining our cause against Eurynomos, should he succeed in his plan. Never have werewolves and vampires been so united. Even humans were joining our side. Now that my brother had succeeded to our father as the vampire Lord, they weren't afraid of us anymore. Humans began being accepted by vampires everywhere. They were allowed to take better jobs than when my father was the ruler. To think he only allowed them to be slaves. I was happy that humans were now free within our lands. Even if it would never give me my mate back. Still, today, I could see everything he did to her in my nightmares. I can still feel the pain from the mate bond breaking. All of that because she was a human, instead of a vampire. I couldn't even save her. I was so angry at myself for not being able to! If only I could turn back time and hold her in my arms once more! I sighed. I needed to focus back on the war to get away from those thoughts. It was the past. There was nothing I could do to change it. I shouldn't keep blaming myself. I did everything I could. She wouldn't want me to hurt myself.

I did the same thing I always do to stop thinking about her. I focused back on the army we were gathering, keeping myself busy. I wanted to rejoice at the thought everyone was uniting against the demon. Still, it was sad that it took a great threat to get everyone to let their prejudices aside and unite. I only hoped that once the demon was eliminated, people would continue to accept each other. My brother was a kind vampire Lord. He wanted peace between our kinds. Especially since Kate was a werewolf. This was the best chance for peace we've had in centuries!

I was startled as someone knocked on the door. A vampire servant was waiting.

"My Prince, Lady Bianca, wishes to see you. She is with Elwin, at his laboratory."

I nodded.

"Thank you very much. I will go see them immediately."

The servant bowed, then left.

I smiled. I liked the fact we had servants instead of slaves at the castle now. It was one of the first rules Damien established when he became the ruler. The slaves were now free. They could stay and work at the castle if they wished, or go find something else to do. Part of them decided to stay. A servant's quarters had been installed in the castle, giving them proper rooms and bedding. They now had access to showers and clean clothes, were fed adequately, and were paid for their services. All things my father had denied them. Furthermore, they were not scared anymore and weren't threatened to be bled to death. Job openings were offered to fill vacancies. Some vampires decided to apply, as the pay was good.

Things were changing for the better. It filled my heart with warmth. It was nice to feel this way. Not so long ago, it was filled with nothing more than sadness, anger, and regret. I took a minute to check that my black shirt was correctly buttoned, just the way I liked it, flowing over my jeans. I wasn't on a royal mission or anything. I didn't need to be formal.

Elwin's laboratory wasn't very far. I knocked on the door.

"Come in," said Elwin. His voice sounded like it came from far inside his laboratory.

I entered and saw that he was at the far end of the room, staring at a big book on a bookstand. Bianca was with him, and she was holding another book, smaller, in her hands. I made my way to them.

"Hi! You wanted to see me?" I asked.

Bianca's face lit up when she saw me. I became friends with her easily. Somehow, it's like

I've known her for centuries, even though we've only met two years ago when my brother found his mate.

"Arius! I'm so happy to see you!" She answered joyfully.

"My Prince," Elwin slightly bowed.

Bianca wasn't one for formalities. She hastily gave the book she was holding to Elwin and came to hug me. I laughed as I watched Elwin's surprised face. This kind of warm friendship was exactly what I needed, and I was happy to return the hug to her.

We broke the hug when we heard Elwin clear his throat.

"Elwin, my friend, you can relax a little bit."

His shoulders somewhat relaxed a little. I couldn't blame him for being so formal. He'd been used to centuries of very strict service under my father's and my grandfather's rules. I wondered if he would eventually adapt to this new type of ruling, or if he'll stay this way forever. Could you teach an old vampire new tricks?

Bianca took the book back from Elwin's hands and showed it to me. It was a vampire book that described the castle's immediate surroundings and lands. The book was open to a page that held a map. This map had little details. It was a very high-level map.

In her other hand, she held another map. This map held many details and looked to have been handmade.

"Arius! I need your help," she started, eagerly.

"What for?" I responded.

"See the lands over to the North? I need you to go to the Moon elves' lands."

I looked at the place she was pointing on the map. It was on the North Shore of Montréal. To be frank, I never ventured over there. I never needed to. And so, I had never met the Moon elves, either. I wondered if they would welcome a vampire on their lands.

"What do you need me to do?"

I was rather curious to know. I only hoped it didn't include any killing.

"See over there?" She pointed to a mountain in the Moon elves' lands. "That is Y'vagroth. It's the highest mountain known in these lands. And it is said to hold a shrine to the Naiad nymphs."

The Naiad nymph… I know I have heard the name before… But for some reason, I couldn't seem to recall. Elwin saw my tilted head while I pondered and answered without me even asking.

"The Naiad nymphs are the nymphs of the water. They reside in springs, rivers, wells. Any body of water they deem worthy of their presence."

Huh, so that's where I've heard that name. It must have been in ancient mythology classes. It wasn't one of my strong subjects, and it's been more than a century ago.

"Thank you for the reminder, Elwin," I answered while rubbing the back of my neck. "Why do you need me to go there?" I asked Bianca.

She smiled.

"I believe that you might be able to find the Angelus Hyssopus over there."

"The... what?"

Bianca giggled.

"The Angel Hyssop. It's a very rare flower."

Bianca then pointed to the big book on the bookstand. Inside the book was a drawing of a flower. It looked beautiful and pure.

"This is the Angelus Hyssopus," started Elwin. "We believe it might hold magical properties that could cure Bianca's father."

My eyes opened wide, and my heart raced at the realization.

"Oh, that is great news!" I exclaimed.

"So, will you go over there to retrieve it?" asked Bianca.

Right, I thought to myself. We needed to retrieve the flower first. Heh, for a second there, I forgot about that part and thought we already had it. I grinned.

"Of course I will!"

Bianca jumped while clapping her hands. I loved her bubbly personality.

"I must warn you, my prince." I looked at Elwin. "The Angelus Hyssopus is very rare. To grow, it needs the low pressure from high altitude, and an abundance of water. That is why we believe the shrine of the Naiad nymphs is a good place to look for it."

I rubbed my chin while thinking. It made sense. This meant I would have to climb a mountain. That shouldn't be too much of a problem. I could probably even fly over to the top if I wasn't too tired from getting all the way there. It also means I'll get to find the Naiad nymphs, that should be interesting.

"Alright, I'll do it," I answered.

"Here." Elwin handed me a piece of cloth and a satchel.

"What is it?" I asked.

"When you cut the flower, you need to wrap it immediately in that cloth, put it in the satchel, and come back as fast as you can," he exhorted.

"Why?"

"Because if you don't, the flower will wither too fast and lose its magic properties."

"That would be a waste of efforts," I stated.

"Indeed," Elwin agreed.

"Okay, I will do this. I know how important it is to find a cure for your father, Bianca."

She pressed her hands on her heart.

"Thank you so much!" she answered.

I loved helping people. It was one of the things I always felt good about. I felt that somehow, by helping people, I could make up for the fact I couldn't protect Mylandra.

"Don't sweat it," I answered. "I'll prepare myself and leave."

They both nodded. I left Elwin's laboratory and made my way to my room to get ready.

I made sure to have a proper meal before leaving and savored a glass of my favorite blood wine. I left first thing in the morning. From the castle, I flew northwest. I passed over the Valley of Nysa, where the war had happened two years ago. Everybody had kept their promise and helped the wood nymphs repair their homes. From the sky, it seemed the valley's greenery had completely returned. On both sides, the majestic mountains remained, their rivers still flowing down to the woods at their base. There was no trace left of the battle that happened two years ago. Really, it was a sight to see.

I continued on my way, a little more to the west than north. After a while, I passed over Montréal. I took care of flying higher in the sky, not wanting to attract unwanted attention. This was a big city, and I preferred small towns and the forest much more. Finally, I crossed over the St.Lawrence River. A little further north was the Moon elves' lands.

I had flown for quite some time and decided it would be better to land. I landed in a small forest in the Moon elves' lands. Goosebumps were sliding along the back of my neck as I watched, in awe, the beauty of this place. The floor was covered in dead tree leaves, layering the path of oranges, reds, yellows, and browns. In the air lingered the scent of decaying leaves, giving it an earthy smell. Bright yellow and orange leaves were left in the trees, showcasing their colors one last time, waiting for the soft touch of a breeze to bring them to the floor. The rays of the sun passing through the trees seemed to have a yellowish color, making them look even brighter. With each breath of the wind, leaves were flying all around me. It felt as if I was inside a snow globe, and somebody just shook it. I was taken by this colorful display of wonders and wondered if these lands were magic. Maybe they were imbued by the elves' magic that lived here?

I started walking in the woods. I soon realized that I had spent a lot of energy flying here. I still had to go all the way to Y'vagroth and go up the mountain. And when, or if, I find the flower, I'll need to fly back as soon as possible to make sure it doesn't wither away. Maybe it would be more cautious to feed before going further. These woods were surely inhabited by a lot of creatures. I should try to find a deer. An animal that size should provide enough blood to replenish me for a long time.

I let my instincts take over me. Suddenly, every sound became crisper. I could hear the sound the bird's wings made while flapping in the air. I saw squirrels fighting in a tree over an acorn. I hid myself as much as I could, hiding my scent and walking silently, so that animals couldn't detect me. From afar, I heard the rustle of leaves as they were crushed by deer hoofs. I turned my head and immediately managed to see a young adult deer walking slowly, a few yards away. The beast was unaware of my presence. It was a beauty, but I needed to feed. It was the constant battle of life, and none could escape it.

I started to stalk the deer, approaching it carefully. Although it was daylight, I was quite good at hiding my presence. Hunting was one of my favorite activities. But I preferred to be careful. I wouldn't want it to run away. I was fast enough to catch a running deer, but it would be easier if I didn't have to run. I focused solely on the beast, shoving out all other sounds to avoid distraction. As I approached, the scent of the deer became stronger, making me hungrier. My fangs started to grow. I waited patiently until I was close to it, coming from behind.

The deer startled as I jumped on it, piercing its hide with my sharp nails. It reared itself, trying to get me off its back, but I was holding fiercely. I didn't wait any further, not wanting the beast to suffer. Sensing the blood pulse in its veins, I immediately sank my teeth into its neck, my fangs finding the veins naturally. It didn't take long for the deer to stop moving and fall to the ground. I was submerged by the sweet taste of the beast's blood.

It didn't have the metallic taste that humans often used to describe blood. I guess it was due to the fact that blood was our primary nutrient. The best way I could describe what it tasted like was to compare it to when you eat a steak that's been half cooked. But obviously, no words could totally justify how good it was to feed from a fresh animal.

I was almost done feeding, wiping dripping blood from my chin, when I heard a cracking sound nearby. In my need to feed, I had let my guards down. I could feel I was the one being stalked. I retracted my nails from the deer I was still holding and got myself back up, scanning the woods to find the source of the sound. Suddenly, a branch cracked behind me. Whatever it was, it was fast. I turned around to catch the glimpse of a shadow running. I didn't even have time to turn around again that I felt something pointy in my back.

"Don't you move," a female voice ordered.

I wanted to turn back and attack. I knew I could probably defeat her anytime I wanted. I mean, I was a vampire prince. I could just send a shockwave of my power through the ground and destabilize her. Or use my hypnotic spell on her mind. I had lots of choices. Yet, something prevented me from doing it.

Her voice sounded like a melody in my hearts. She smelled like lilac flowers. My mind was racing. I couldn't understand what was happening to me. What was that feeling? How could it be possible? This didn't make sense! You can only have one mate in your life… And Mylandra died years ago, by my father's hands. What sort of sorcery was this?

"Hey! Are you listening?" said the female voice behind me. By her tone, she was annoyed.

"Huh, sorry I wasn't paying attention," I answered apologetically.

"Well, you'd better listen when your life's on the line. Now, turn around slowly, as I asked!"

I chuckled to myself, not letting it show so that I wouldn't insult her. If only she knew the extent of my power, she'd know that my life wasn't in danger.

I raised my hands, and did as she asked, turning myself slowly until I faced her.

I had to refrain myself from gasping so much she was beautiful. She was an elf. That's for sure, you couldn't mistake those kinds of ears. And since I was on the Moon elves' territory that meant she was a Moon elf as well. Her skin was white, but still to a less extent than my own, with a slight blue hue to it. She had deep piercing blue eyes and had long blond hair with slight waves in it. I could easily see myself getting lost in those eyes of hers.

As she studied me, I was wondering if she was feeling the same thing as me. I was still so confused as to how this was possible. Could it be that maybe, maybe Fate decided that what happened to me and Mylandra was too cruel, and that I was given a second chance at love? Maybe it wasn't a fated love? But just love at first sight? The only way I could know if it was a fated love would be if we could communicate through our minds. But for this to happen, we needed to get closer. Only then will I know if our bond is the same one as fated mates. And right now, it didn't look like this could happen.

"Who are you? What are you doing on our lands?"

I lowered my hands to answer, but she immediately pointed her two short swords at me. She was a dual wielder. This needed much agility and coordination! Not many people can dually wield weapons. I put my hands back in the air. I wouldn't want her to think I was going to attack her.

"I meant no threat, my lady. I only meant to present myself."

She lowered her swords.

"Try anything funny and you'll regret it."

I nodded to her then proceeded to lower my hands.

"My name is Arius. I am a vampire prince, at your service," I slightly bowed at her.

"A vampire? What the hell is a vampire doing on my people's territory?" she asked, frightened.

"Please, I mean no harm. I am looking for a very rare flower. For you see, a friend of mine is greatly sick, and I've heard that this flower might be his only hope of recovering."

Her eyes narrowed as she was taking in what I had just said. I knew she was studying me, assessing whether or not she could trust me.

"What flower are you looking for?"

I froze for a moment. I didn't quite remember the name of the flower. I mean, I knew the way it looked. I was good at remembering faces or how things looked. But I sucked at remembering names. I had to repeat names of people multiple times before I remembered them.

"Huh, I think it was called the Angely… Angelo… no that's not it. Angelus? Oh yes, that sounds right. Anyway, I'm not sure what the name of the flower was, but I remember I need to go to the top of that mountain over there." I pointed to the mountain behind her.

"All the way up Y'vagroth?" she asked in disbelief.

"Yes, I am to find the shrine of the Naiads. The flower is believed to be growing over there."

The woman seemed to ponder a bit.

"That's problematic."

"Why?"

"That means you will need to cross over a good part of my people's territory and climb our holy mountain."

I could feel she sounded conflicted.

"Please. I only need one flower to heal my friend. I will be on my way afterwards."

Well, of course, I would prefer to stay. Now that I've met her, I would love to get to know her more. But I couldn't tell her that.

"I cannot let you go there alone. No one can get on the holy mountain but our people."

I felt sad about her decision. Yet, there was no way I was letting down Bianca, Kate, and Will. I will get that flower, with or without the Moon elves' permission. I was not sure how I could manage to get away from her without hurting her, and still go to the mountain. This would be difficult.

Her voice got me out of my thoughts.

"But… Your cause is noble. I would gladly make the journey with you, making sure you only take your flower and leave. This is the only offer you will get. Take it or leave our lands now."

I rejoiced. This was a way better option! It also meant I could spend time with her! I mean, I know I wasn't here to find myself a girlfriend. But I hadn't felt this way for centuries. Although she didn't show any signs that she was attracted to me, I couldn't let this chance slip through my fingers.

"That would be fantastic!" I answered, laughing a little.

She smiled for the first time at my comment. I was blown away by the beauty of her smile.

"Great, it's a deal then!"

She finally lowered her weapons and signaled for me to follow her.

"Might I know your name? I will know how to call you."

"My name is Elashor. I am a warden of the Moon elves."

I repeated her name in my head. Elashor, what a beautiful name. I would make sure not to forget it, repeating it as much as I needed. She was already a few steps ahead of me when she turned back.

"Are you coming? No one must see us. Outsiders normally require a formal permission to enter our territory. And the Queen would never allow an outsider to go to Y'vagroth."

I nodded and proceeded to follow her, understanding she was bending the rules for me.

Chapter 6 (Leila)

A foul stench

I woke up early and put on a pair of jeans with a simple shirt. It was my time to do the patrol of the pack's lands. This was one of my favorite things to do. I loved to run in the forest, got to see the animals, the plants, feel the magic force of nature at its fullest. As always, Skye would come with me. This always turned into friend confessions as we walked. I loved to be able to spend this time with my bestie.

My grandma was already up and doing her chieftess' duties when I got down. I hugged her and got outside to meet Skye in front of her home. She was already there, waiting for me. I knew she would have preferred not to do these patrols. Skye didn't like to walk much. I think she preferred to sit and drink coffee all the time. But every member of the pack needed to give a hand. This was one of the easiest jobs in the pack, so she didn't complain too much.

"Hi Leila!"

Skye was already coming to hug me with a big smile on her face.

"Skye!"

We broke into a hug. She might have some flaws, like everyone, but I loved my best friend so much!

"Are you ready to do this?"

She pouted her mouth at my question.

"Do we really have to?"

I giggled at her answer.

"You know we have to."

I winked at her, then motioned for us to get going. She giggled too while following me.

"Yes, I know, you're right."

We started walking, already talking together.

"Did you hear about Marc?"

"No, what?"

"He broke up with Sylvia."

"No way! How come?"

"Some people say he cheated on her!!"

"No way!!! He would never do that!"

Skye always knew all the gossips of the pack, and even some of the human towns nearby. I didn't know she managed to be aware of everything going on everywhere all the time. With all the tasks I had to do, I didn't have time to speak with everyone.

Speaking with Skye allowed me to keep updated on everything faster than to talk with everyone. She was my own little concentrated social media.

We ventured to the west of the pack's territory while she rambled about the gossips on Marc. He was a fine man, and I was sure most of this gossip was grossly exaggerated, but Skye loved to be dramatic about things. I smelled something foul, something I had never smelled before. It was subtle, and Skye couldn't smell it, since she had no wolf in her. But my wolf smelled it very well. I stopped walking.

"What? What is it?"

Skye was used to this. She knew that if I suddenly stopped; it was surely because something was wrong. I was trying to figure out where the smell was coming from. It was a windy fall morning, but I was able to figure it out easily despite these winds.

"There." I pointed towards the coniferous trees in front of us. She nodded.

We started venturing carefully. As we advanced, we started seeing dead animals lying on the floor. They looked like they were killed not long ago, but they didn't seem to have any wounds. Did the source of this wicked stench kill them?

The more we advanced, the stronger the stench was. All the flowers and forest herbs were withered and blackened. The trees were dry, and branches had fallen to the ground, layering the path with broken pieces everywhere.

"What the hell happened here?" asked Skye.

I shrugged my shoulders.

"I don't know, but I'm getting the feeling we're getting close," I whispered back at her.

We soon arrived at a strange grotto. The strangest thing was, I was sure this cave was not there before. I knew our territory so well, for having patrolled it many times. This didn't make sense! Caverns don't just appear out of nowhere!

But whatever was killing the animals, it came from this cave. The smell was so strong here that Skye and I had to pinch our nose. I wanted to go look inside. I was about to throw up because the smell was so strong. Skye put her hand on my shoulder.

"Leila, if those animals were killed by this smell, or by whatever creature that emits the smell, we shouldn't venture in there."

She was right. The best thing to do was to alert my grandmother. We were a pack. We needed to decide together what to do about this.

"Yes, you're right, Skye. Let's get back to the pack."

We turned back and started running together, holding hands, like when we were little. Younger, Skye was clumsy and tended to trip on tree roots coming out of the ground. I had taken the habit of holding her hand when we were running to avoid her stumbling down and hurting herself. I started doing this when we were little, and never stopped doing it, even if she was way less clumsy today than when she was as a child.

We ran as fast as Skye could manage to run, staying together. We were back in no time to the pack's house.

"Ravynne!" Skye screamed as we entered the house.

My grandmother was drinking her tea. She looked at us with a worried look in her eyes.

"What is it?"

"We found a cave on the territory. I know it sounds crazy, but this cave was not there yesterday. And from it came a wicked stench. All around, animals and plants were dead," I answered.

My grandmother's mouth went agape, and she dropped the cup she was holding in her hand. The cup fell to the ground and shattered, dropping its content on the floor. But my grandmother didn't seem to care, as she raised her hand to her mouth.

"Oh, dear Moon Goddess, have mercy on us!"

Skye and I stared at my grandmother, not really knowing what to think of her reaction. Surely, she knew something we didn't.

"What is it?" I asked her, as Skye and I wiped the floor and picked up the shattered cup. She vaguely stared at the spilled tea, then at us.

"Oh Skye! Oh Leila, my treasure. This is bad, this is so bad! Our ancestors foretold this day! We need help! We cannot manage this alone."

"Manage what?" Skye asked.

My grandmother took a few seconds to gather her thoughts.

"The demon is coming."

Skye and I exchanged an incredulous look.

"The… demon?" I asked.

My grandmother nodded.

"Don't you remember the origins of our pack?"

I thought back to the stories told about our pack. I couldn't recall anything about a demon. While I thought about it, I realized she barely ever talked about the origins of the pack. I looked at Skye, but she shook her head, meaning she didn't remember anything about it either.

I cleared my throat.

"Grandma, I'm sorry. I listen when you give classes, but I don't recall you talking about the origins of the pack or a demon."

She let out a deep breath.

"Oh, my dear, you are right. I don't really like to speak about it and only the oldest members of the pack remember this."

She rose from her seat and started putting a bag together.

"I think it's time I tell you. But it is a long story. And I'm afraid we're lacking time right now. The only thing I'll say is that our pack's ancestors were in charge of keeping an ancient demon sealed away in the underworld."

Skye and I gasped at this information.

"So… When you said the demon is coming… You meant this one?" I asked.

My grandmother nodded.

"Yes, and we won't be able to face him alone. We need help."

She stepped towards the door and motioned for us to follow.

"Where are we going?" Skye asked.

"We are going to the nearest pack. We need some help with this demon."

I froze at these words, and my heart tightened. The nearest pack. That's where he lived. My wolf longed to get back there ever since last night when I saw him. He almost marked me. As much as my wolf wanted this, I wasn't about to let an asshole that already has a mate mark me. I couldn't deny the mate bond. I was even able to talk to him through his mind. Even if we didn't even kiss. Our wolves met, and they were both thrilled. I've barely slept the last few days as much as I was thinking of him. Going there would probably be hurtful. His scent will surely be so much stronger. I know I'll have a hard time to refrain myself from finding him. I'll try to just stick to the task at hand and ignore it as much as I can.

We started walking in the direction of the other pack's land, to the southeast. This path I now knew almost by heart. I've returned so many times. I couldn't help myself; it was just too strong. For heaven's sake! I even still had that piece of jean with his scent in my bag. How pathetic could I get? I hated this bond. If only he rejected me, we could be over this already.

"Are you okay?" asked Skye. I nodded.

"Yes, I'll manage."

"He lives there, doesn't he?"

I swallowed a lump in my throat. "Yes," I whispered in a broken voice.

Skye put her arm around my shoulders, comforting me.

"It's okay, we'll be with you."

I felt a little better knowing I wasn't alone.

We were in their pack's territory for a few minutes only, when a man came to see us. He looked like he was old. He wore a tiled flannel shirt with a loose jean.

"What are you doing on our pack's territory?" He asked with a strong voice. He didn't seem happy to see us.

My grandmother took a step towards him.

"I am Ravynne, chieftess of the Hands of Fate pack. Who are you?"

"Chieftess? I have never heard of that title before."

"We do not abide by the rules of the Alpha. We have our own rules," she said defiantly to the man.

"Oh… I see. You're from the rogues' pack. My name is Marcus. I am an advisor here in the pack of the Southern Forest."

"I need to speak to your Alpha. We're in a dire situation."

Marcus seemed to be evaluating if he trusted us or not. I could sense his wolf being wary. He seemed to be taking in our scent before deciding.

"Alright, follow me. Don't you dare to betray me."

My grandmother nodded.

"We would never."

We followed Marcus and soon were in the middle of the pack's town. I had never come here. Small wooden houses were everywhere. It felt less connected to nature than my pack, but it felt beautiful anyway.

"I don't like it here," Skye whispered to me.

"It's not that bad," I answered. I liked it, it seemed like every pack member had their little house and could live happily.

As we approached, my wolf began to be uneasy. She was restless. She wanted out and I barely could keep her in check. She was screaming "mate" all over again in my head. I wondered where he was. I didn't expect his scent to be this strong. It was intoxicating me, and I just wanted to find him so bad! I dug my nails into my hands, trying to remind myself that I needed to stick with my grandmother and Skye.

We finally arrived at the pack's house. Marcus knocked at the door.

A woman with red hair answered the door. She had a pretty blue dress, and her deep green eyes were studying us.

I didn't really care about her. What knocked me out was how strong his scent was once the door was opened. Surely, he was working at the pack's house. Maybe he was a Beta? Or an advisor? This wasn't good. I had hoped to stay away from him, but it seems things wouldn't go the way I thought they would.

"My Luna," Marcus bowed to her. "I found these rogue wolves on our territory. They ask to speak to the Alpha."

"Thank you, Marcus," she answered, keeping her head high. "I shall fetch him. You can all enter and wait in the lobby."

She turned around and began walking inside the pack's house. I wondered why she didn't call him through their mate bond. It was faster than walking up to her mate. We would be done faster, and I could get away from that enticing scent. The sooner the better, as I didn't know how much I could keep my wolf in check.

We entered the lobby, and I only hoped he wouldn't show up. Maybe he didn't know I was there. That was a foolish thought. The mate bond was so strong. It was certain he knew I was there. Hopefully, he would decide to stay hidden and wait for me to leave.

I was looking at pictures on the wall of past Alphas and their pups. I loved those old black and white pictures. I heard steps behind me, and my heart jumped. It was him; I knew it without even turning back.

"My Alpha, there you are," Marcus said.

I froze. Did he say… Alpha? This wasn't good… Oh, so that's why the Luna couldn't call him through their mate bond… He said she wasn't a fated mate. Of course, because I was his fated mate… That means, I was meant to be a Luna. The thoughts were racing through my mind. I couldn't think straight anymore. I was overwhelmed by so many emotions at the same time.

"Leila, would you please show the Alpha some respect?" I was startled at my grandmother's voice.

She didn't know he was my mate. Neither did Skye.

Slowly, I turned around. There he was, with his beautiful blue eyes and dark brown hair. His broad muscled chest showing through his shirt. My heart was beating strong in my chest. The way he was looking at me, I knew he felt it, too. This was surely as hard for him as it was for me.

His Luna was pressing at his side. Her hand was around his arm. Just the sight of her touching him made my wolf jump. I had to hold back a growl that wanted to come out. It was pure jealousy. My wolf wanting to protect what was rightfully hers, given by the Moon goddess. I had the hardest time doing it, but I managed to. Any signs of hostility would be seen as a direct attack. We needed their help against the demon if I was to believe what my grandmother said.

I watched him; he was still looking at me. I felt he was looking directly at my soul through his gaze. I wondered how he managed to keep this calm, despite the mate bond pulling at him.

"It's an honor to meet you, Alpha Will," my grandmother started.

"The honor is mine. What can I do for you?"

"We need to speak."

"Come," he gestured. "Let us go into my study."

We all followed him further into the pack's house. I watched as his Luna and he held hands while walking. I couldn't help myself but to think at how I wished to tear that hand away from his. It took all my energy to keep my wolf calm. This would be way harder than I had anticipated.

I was following Elashor through the woods. Following might not be the right word. Admiring her beauty was more accurate. For every step she took, every swing of her hips, she was making my heart beat stronger.

"I meant to tell you sooner, but thank you very much for your help, Elashor."

She looked at me with her radiant smile.

"It's only natural to help you, Arius."

Hearing her say my name made me the happiest man, even if it was only by saying something as trivial.

"Stay close to me. I wouldn't want you to get lost."

I chuckled lowly. She wouldn't have to ask me twice. I closed the distance between us. I was now close enough to grab her hand should I want to. The only thing that bothered me was that I had no idea what she thought of me. I was a vampire, and she was an elf. I've always thought elves were higher creatures. Not that vampires were not good.

I mean, as a vampire prince, I knew very well how powerful we could be. But vampires didn't have the best reputation amongst other races. This was my first encounter with the elves, and I wasn't really sure what to think of it.

I cleared my throat, not really sure how to start the conversation.

"Elashor, I… I wanted to know something." She looked at me, and for a moment, I could see my reflection in her eyes.

"Yes?"

"Hum, well. I was wondering. Aren't you afraid?"

"Afraid of what?"

"Well… You know, I'm a vampire."

"Oh, right!" She blushed at my question. "Well, I have to say, it's my first time meeting a vampire. And I have to admit that the things I had heard about your race were not the most… flattering. Seeing you feed on that deer was… interesting."

Of course, it wasn't. Only the worst stories cross the borders. You can have one crazy person in a race, and that's enough for everyone to think you're all like that. Who hadn't heard of Dracula? That guy was deranged! It took us years to be able to capture him and put an end to the reign of terror he had. By then, the damage had already been done.

We tried to do diplomacy for years to fix what he had broken.

"But I have to say, you're not as frightening as I thought vampires were. I'm enjoying your presence."

That last part warmed my heart.

"Well, not everyone is as bad as what they say," I said awkwardly. She giggled a little. I didn't really understand why, but I seemed to lose all my composure because of her. I feel like I'm clumsy and fail to think straight.

"What I meant to say is, I'm also enjoying your presence." That's better, I thought to myself. Elashor seemed happy by my answer as well.

We continued our march towards Y'vagroth, while talking about simple things, trying to get to know each other better.

Chapter 7 (Arius)

Y'vagroth

We finally arrived at the base of a mountain. It was majestic, and the top of it was lost in the clouds. I was amazed by the grandeur of this mountain. I could feel a power emanating from the center of it. It was as if it commanded respect.

"This is Y'vagroth, Arius."

I took a moment to admire its splendor. My eyes then met those of Elashor, which were far more marvelous than the mountain. How I wish I could tell her how I felt. Even though we just met… this was crazy. I had only felt like that once, and it was when I met Mylandra, my mate. All those years since her death, I thought I would never feel like that anymore. All my life I've been told, you only get one mate. I've felt so devastated when she was killed. Yet, for the first time in centuries, I felt free from this grief. I was truly happy, and ready to let my heart love again. I felt the nervousness of not knowing what she thought about me. I felt butterflies in my stomach at the thought of telling her what I yearned.

I stared deeply into her eyes.

"This is the most beautiful thing I have ever seen."

I wasn't talking about the mountain, but I liked how ambiguous it sounded. That way, I could get out of it, depending on her reaction. Which I wouldn't have to, since I'm pretty sure I saw her blush a little.

"Shall we climb?" I asked, taking a few steps forward.

She nodded and followed me.

The base of the mountain wasn't too steep. However, the mountain quickly became steeper as we climbed. Soon, it was as if we were climbing rocky stairs. We soon found ourselves in deep fog. I was guessing we were now at the level of the clouds. I hadn't realized this mountain was so high, nor that getting to the top would be this hard. I had originally thought about flying up, but I didn't plan on meeting with Elashor. Now that I've met her, flying was out of the question. The fog was so dense; it was hard to see her. Luckily, with my vampire instinct, I could easily sense her heartbeat, hear the blood pumping in her veins. I just felt it naturally through my body, like a second sense.

We were still in thick fog when I heard a grunt, followed by a high-pitched shriek. I wasn't sure who or what made the grunt, but I knew for sure the shriek came from Elashor.

"Arius!" Her cry came from the air.

I flew up and followed the sound of her voice, as the fog was so thick, I could barely see anything. I finally saw her and realized she was held by a giant hand.

"Elashor! What's happening?"

"Arius, help!" she only pleaded.

I detected a movement coming from behind me and swerved just in time to avoid it. It was another hand. What on heart could be this big? I asked myself.

I continued my way up further until I was able to see its face. In front of me, I could see a very big, bald head. In its forehead was one giant protruding eye. A cyclops! What did a cyclops do on this mountain? Nobody said anything about a cyclops! How the hell was I supposed to get rid of that? And without having Elashor being killed in the process?

I didn't want to lose another woman I loved without even having told her what I felt!

The cyclops grunted at my sight and tried to catch me with its free hand. I easily avoided it. I realized that it might be very tall and strong, but I was way faster and more agile than him. We played that game a few times, and each time, I was able to avoid him. My vampire senses allowed me to easily sense every movement the creature made. On another hand, the thick fog was probably making it hard for the creature to see. I had the upper hand.

After a few failed attempts, the creature seemed like it was tired of trying to catch me, and he began walking away, with Elashor still in his hand.

I heard her shriek, and I realized that the cyclops had decided it wanted to eat her. There was no way I was letting that happen. I grabbed as big of a boulder I could lift. Vampires normally have a lot of strength, so it was actually a very big boulder. I flew up to the cyclops' head, over his eye, and dropped the boulder directly into his eye.

The creature screeched with pain. As it did, it released Elashor to grab its eye with his hands. As soon as he did, Elashor began to fall to the ground, as she couldn't fly, like me. I descended as fast as I could and managed to catch her before she hit the floor. She held on to me tight and tucked her head in the crook of my neck. My heart was beating strong from that connection with her, but I knew cyclops were strong creatures. It would be only a matter of seconds before it would try to catch us again.

Taking advantage of the fog, I flew a little up the mountain, still with Elashor in my arms, holding her tight. Finally, I saw a small dent in the rock, creating a small cavern. Small enough that a cyclops couldn't enter it, but big enough for us to hide inside it and be hidden from plain sight. I made way in the cave and gestured at Elashor to stay quiet. She nodded nervously, still shaking.

The ground shook from the weight of the cyclops as he walked by, searching for us. We didn't move. I think I barely allowed myself to breathe, afraid the creature would hear us. We listened, as each step was either going further or coming back towards us. I was grateful for the fog outside, or he would have seen us otherwise. After a while, the steps began going further down the mountain, down the path we had taken to climb the mountain. We stayed like that, hidden, not moving, for I don't know how long. When we didn't hear any steps anymore, and felt it was safe, we began moving again.

That's only then that I realized that I was still holding Elashor in my arms. In the midst of the moment, I hadn't released her from my embrace. She was leaning against me and seemed to be enjoying the moment. I could feel the warmth of her body against mine. I could feel her heartbeat through mine. I was enjoying this moment way more than I wanted to admit it. Could it be love at first sight? Would it be possible that Fate had granted me a second mate?

I suddenly felt nervous. I didn't really know how I was supposed to react, what I was supposed to say. Should I just release her from my embrace? Or stay this way? The earlier rescue justified my embrace, but now that she was safe, I didn't know what to do…

"I didn't know vampires could fly," she whispered, looking into my eyes. I flushed from the way she stared at me.

"Yes, we can."

"That's very useful."

"It can be, but it also takes a lot of our strength, so we don't overdo it."

She nodded and smiled.

"Thanks for saving me."

I smiled back at her.

"I wasn't about to let you be eaten away by that creature."

She pondered for a moment.

"You could have. Then you would have been free to go wherever you wanted into our territory."

Her words hit me. She was right, but I would never do that.

"That thought didn't even cross my mind."

I put her back on the ground, reluctantly letting go of my embrace. The moment seemed perfect for it. She didn't say anything about the fact I had held her for so long, which I was grateful for.

"I didn't know a cyclops lived here," I stated.

Elashor hesitated, "well… I think we might have angered the Oreads…"

I repeated, "The Oreads?"

She nodded. "Yes, they are the mountain nymphs. I told you, this mountain is sacred. Only my people are usually allowed to climb this mountain. I think we might have angered them."

I thought all the nymphs were friendly creatures. But then again, maybe I was mistaken?

This was my first time in elven territory, so there might be a few things I didn't understand.

"Do you think it's safe if we continue to the top?"

Elashor looked up while pondering.

"Well, I think it should be safe. I mean, even if we did anger them by coming here, I don't think it will be worse if we continue on."

Right, I thought. I only hoped there wouldn't be hordes of monsters and creatures chasing us all the way up to the top of the mountain.

"Okay, shall we be on our way, then?"

She nodded, and we carefully looked outside to see if it was safe. The fog was still there. I bet this part of the mountain was always covered in fog. It was so high; it was as if all the clouds had got caught in it.

We made our way past the clouds and the fog, and to my relief, the cyclops was nowhere to be seen. I guess it went back down and renounced to find us. We were now so high that even birds didn't come this high. We were surrounded by silence, and the light from the sun shining without any resistance. There were no plants, we were walking on rock only.

We were walking silently, admiring the beauty of this place. I was feeling like I was walking on sacred ground. Further ahead, a rock wall was standing in front of us. I began hearing water flowing. I didn't understand… We were above the clouds. How could there be water at this altitude? Was I losing my mind?

"Do you hear that?" I asked Elashor, doubtful.

She giggled a little. "We're here," she motioned to the rock wall with her hand.

I frowned, not understanding what she meant.

She motioned for me to go forward, so I did.

I was taken aback by what I saw on the other side of the rock wall. At the center of this deserted place stood a small waterfall, seeming to flow from nothingness. The water fell down into this vat dug into the rock itself. On the sides of the vat grew a few shrubs and flowers, nourished by the water falling from the waterfall. I had no idea where this water came from. I guessed the answer was that it came from the magic of the creatures that bathed in it.

Inside of it. I could see some creatures, they looked like women made of water. They looked like they held shape, but you could see through them. They would disappear when going under the water, and yet, I could hear them talk and laugh together. Their hair was flowing through the air as they moved their heads. I stayed there, watching, not making a sound. I was still far away but didn't want to interrupt.

I was startled when a hand landed on my arm. I looked down to see Elashor.

"Those are the Naiads, the water nymphs."

I nodded, "That's what I thought."

"Are you ready to find your flower?"

Right, that's the whole reason I came here, didn't I?

"Yes, that was the idea…"

Elashor studied me. "You don't seem convinced anymore. Don't you have someone dear to heal?"

I nodded. "Yes. It's just that I've only just discovered this place, and your people. I feel I have so much to discover."

She smiled. "I understand. Come."

We went forward. The nymphs stopped playing and turned to us.

"What are you doing on our lands, creature of darkness?" They asked, looking at me.

"My name is Arius. I am seeking the Angelus flower. I need to heal a friend that's grievously sick."

One of the nymphs nodded, before adding.

"It is not normally allowed for an outsider to grab a hold of such a powerful reagent."

This was a problem. I didn't intend of leaving this place without the flower. But I didn't want to fight them. God only knew what force these creatures held. I had faith in my own strength, as a vampire prince. But at the same time, there was Elashor. I didn't really want to come here and fight her gods… or whatever these creatures represented to her.

Before I could try to protest, Elashor spoke.

"Please… He's not a creature of darkness. He's good, I saw it."

The nymph looked at her, questioning her words.

"How can I trust your words? Didn't you betray your clan by bringing him here?"

Elashor looked at the ground, fidgeting with her hands. I grabbed her hand. She raised her head and smiled at me. Then looked back at the nymph.

"I know he is good. He saved my life. He fought a cyclops to save me."

She said it with so much strength and determination. It made me happy she truly believed that I was good.

The nymphs concerted with themselves, then turned back to us.

"Alright, we decided to allow you to take one of the Angeluses Hyssopus. You will have only one. Use it wisely."

Relief came upon me at hearing those words. The nymph pointed to a beautiful white flower that grew on the side of the vat. I stepped forward.

One of the nymphs warned me. Her voice seemed to flow through the air.

"You do know that once you pick it up, you will need to act fast before its powers dissipate?"

I nodded to her.

"Yes, I will be on my way after picking it up."

I hid the fact that it tore my heart apart to leave. I wanted to stay with Elashor. She was the most precious person to me, even if she didn't know it. She did what I thought was impossible. She made the sadness of losing my first mate go away. And made me believe in love again. I didn't want to lose her, and I didn't know how to tell her. I was running out of time.

I was hastily searching for something to say to her. But I couldn't find anything. My heart seemed to know what to say, but my brain was blank. Not finding anything, I took a step towards the flower.

A warm hand grabbed mine, the touch of her hand made my heart churn even more. I turned my head to see Elashor, tears silently dripping on her cheeks.

"Please… don't go."

I stepped closer to her, wiping the tears from her cheeks. I didn't understand where this was coming from. I didn't dare to believe the thoughts that came to my mind. I was afraid to even think about it and be heartbroken if they weren't true.

I looked at her blue eyes, losing myself in their beauty for a moment.

"I thought you wanted me gone from your lands after I found the flower."

She slowly nodded. "Yes… but that was… before."

I didn't dare finish that sentence myself, so I asked, "before what?"

She searched through my eyes. It seemed as if she was looking for an answer. Instead of answering, she raised herself on her tiptoes and brought her hands behind my neck, forcing me down to meet her lips. I closed my eyes, tasting her sweet lips. If I was dreaming, then I never wanted to wake up. I put my arms around her hips and brought her closer to me. I felt like it was the first breath I took after so many years.

When we stopped kissing she stepped just an inch from me, to look at me. She seemed to still have questions on her mind. I wasn't sure what to say. What words cannot answer, the heart can. I brought my lips to hers and kissed her back, passionately, her lips parting and our tongues dancing together.

I didn't know exactly how long we kissed, but at one point, we both needed to take a breath of air. We broke the kiss, but I kept her in my arms, not wanting to let her go. I finally decided to tell her everything my heart has been wanting me to.

"Elashor, I know it might sound crazy. I mean, I just met you… But I feel like I've known you for years…"

She smiled as she listened to my rambling. I was nervous. I didn't know exactly how to speak or where I was going. The thoughts seemed so clear. And yet, I was searching for my words as they slipped from me. I felt like an idiot, but at least she wasn't laughing.

"What I mean to say is… Elashor… I think I'm in love with you. So, so in love, it's even mad to think that I could go away and live without you."

Elashor hugged me tightly in her arms and whispered, "oh Arius! I love you too."

Tears were falling down her cheeks again, but they were tears of joy this time. Soon, I began to cry too. It was such a relief to know she felt the same. I felt like I could finally come to terms with my past and look to the future.

Elashor added, "I'm not really sure how it can be possible to love you so much in such a short amount of time."

"I believe that you might be my mate."

Elashor had a questioning look. "Your mate"?

I nodded. "Fate grants us one mate, one person, to love forever."

She smiled. "Oh okay, I understand. Our people call them soulmates."

"I want to know everything about you and your people."

I heard the nymphs behind us. I turned around to see the nymph gesturing for me to grab the flower and got reminded of my task.

"But I really need to bring back this flower first."

Elashor looked disappointed. "I understand."

"I promise to you. After I deliver the flower, I will come back to you."

I grabbed her chin and kissed her one last time, enjoying the warmth of her body against mine, my heart beating fast.

When we separated, I finally made my way to the flower. Gently, I picked it and immediately wrapped it in the cloth Elwin gave me and put it inside the satchel.

I took flight and went straight for the castle, as Elwin instructed me to.

Chapter 8 (Will)

Living Energy

We all sat in my study. I kept Jane close by my side. On the other side of the massive wooden desk were sitting Leila, Skye and Ravynne. I had the hardest time listening to their story. All I could think about was how intoxicating Leila's scent was. I kept thinking back to the other day, when we ran together in the forest in our wolf form. How my wolf was ready to mark her, just like that. She was my everything. I needed her like I needed to breathe. I held Jane's hand, trying to remind myself that she was my Luna. She was the one I chose. I couldn't change my mind just like that. That's why I had tried so hard not to think of Leila in the past few days. I tried so hard to get away from her, but I was feeling miserable. Jane squeezed my hand, and I realized I was lost in my mind again.

"What do you think we should do, Alpha Will?" asked Ravynne.

Sincerely, I hadn't followed what was said. I was too busy trying to resist the mate bond and keeping my wolf in check. Luckily, Jane caught on to the fact I hadn't been listening and filled in the conversation for me.

"This foul stench is definitely a problem. If it kills all animals and plants, it will surely spread all the way here, eventually. Do you agree Will?" She waited for my approval. Once again, I was happy she was there. She filled her Luna responsibilities perfectly.

I watched as Leila rolled her eyes. Nobody else saw it. They were all looking at me, waiting for my answer. But I could feel how Leila was annoyed through our mate bond. I watched how she twitched slightly and fiddled with her fingers every time Jane spoke. I knew she wasn't doing it on purpose. My wolf would do the same, or even worse, if some male was to approach her the same way Jane was by my side. I bit my lip, feeling bad for putting her through this. She was the most wonderful woman I had ever seen. She deserved to be happy and have a loving mate.

Looking up, I realized I still hadn't answered anything. I cleared my throat.

"You are right. We cannot afford to sit still and do nothing. What did you say again was the cause of this stench?"

Ravynne smiled. "I believe this stench is coming from a gate to the underworld opening."

I startled at that last sentence. Could it be that Eurynomos was finally succeeding with his plan? I'll have to ask Bianca when she comes back from the castle with Kate. I've been told they had some encouraging news and needed to go there as soon as possible.

"Why would you think it was a gate to the underworld?" Jane asked.

"Our ancestors were once in charge of keeping an ancient demon sealed away in the underworld. It has been foretold that one day, he would come to this world."

"This demon," I started. "Would he be named Eurynomos?"

Ravynne put a hand on her mouth. "How did you?"

This was interesting. Surely, if their ancestors oversaw keeping Eurynomos sealed away, my sister would surely be eager to meet them.

"We're also having our own problems with this demon. I think you should stay for a while. There's someone I would like you to meet, but she's not here at the moment."

Ravynne and Skye nodded. As for Leila, she had her mouth agape. I knew exactly what she thought, and I shared the same opinion. I had no idea how I would manage to have her that close to me for a few days.

I turned to Jane. "Please ask the maid to prepare a room for our guests. The second one from the entrance will do."

It was the furthest room from my room that was unoccupied. I couldn't manage to be in the same room as her. I was lucky I was able to keep my wolf in check for that long. And now, I really needed to get away from her.

"I'm sorry. I have other things to attend."

Ravynne answered, "thank you for your kindness, Alpha Will."

I couldn't wait anymore. My wolf was screaming at me to claim her. I stood from my seat, trying to keep as calm as I could. I needed to walk to the other side of the desk to get to the door, but they were still sitting on their chairs. Passing this close to Leila, I swear I felt the air becoming hotter. As I neared the door, I heard a gasp. I turned around, but Skye and Ravynne were talking with Jane. Was I dreaming? Maybe I heard it through my mate bond. I watched as Leila's deep chocolate brown eyes were fixated on me. I felt there were so many things she wanted to say but didn't. I knew she could speak to me through our mate bond. Why wasn't she doing it right now? I couldn't stay here and wait to know, as I could barely restrain myself from kissing her. I left the room and went outside. I only hoped that my sister would come back home soon.

I came as fast as I could when I heard Arius was back! This was so exciting!!! And knowing the power of the flower would wither away fast if we didn't take care of it soon enough, there was no time to waste, especially since my father's health had been worsening. It seemed like he's getting weaker with every day that passed. We still didn't know what was slowly killing him, but a thought passed through my mind… I read in a book somewhere in the library that demons could affect the world of the living without being in it. That got me thinking… Could what was happening to my father be related to the demon somehow? I wanted to talk to Steven about that and know his opinion, but for now, he was still busy with Zach and Lilith, preparing the army. I missed his arms right now, but we had so many things to do. I was eager for everything to be done so I could spend more time with my mate.

I was still in the castle's library. It was way bigger than the one we had at the pack's house. There were rows of books on each side of the vast room. The books went up to the ceiling. It was at least two stories high. At the center of the room was a vast open space with multiple tables for people to sit down and read. Despite having some light switches, I loved the old vibe it gave when I lit the chandeliers instead. I avoided lighting the modern lights as much as I could. Some of the books probably hadn't been read in centuries, judging from the amount of dust that covered them. Rolling ladders were embedded into the bookshelves. It was easy to roll yourself up to another book you wanted to check. In the air lingered the distinctive sweet, musky smell of old books that I loved so much. Somehow, it reminded me of coffee or chocolate. I spent most of my time here when I came to the castle. It was my home away from home. Anyway, for now, I needed to rush to Elwin's laboratory. I left the books I was reading on one of the wooden tables and made my way there.

I could hear Elwin's voice even before opening the door. He seemed to have a lively conversation. I didn't eavesdrop; I was way too excited to see what was going on. I entered the room and didn't even look around the usual clutter. I made my way directly to the back of the room, where Arius and Elwin were chatting. A few vials were arranged on a table beside them. Arius held a cloth in his hands.

"Magnificent! Even more beautiful than I thought!" exclaimed Elwin.

Arius was grinning beside him.

As I approached, I could see this beautiful, delicate flower in the cloth Arius was holding. It had hundreds of small white flowers and somehow looked so pure it was almost glowing.

"Wow! Arius, it's beautiful!" I spoke.

"Yes, I know. It wasn't easy to get," he added.

"Right!" Elwin said, as if remembering something. "We must hurry."

I was surprised at how delicately he took the flower. I didn't expect the old sorcerer to be able to take it with such care. I guess that even after all this time, this vampire could still surprise me.

He took the flower and put it in a big glass flask with water in it. I was rather curious to know what he would do with it.

"What's that glass flask for?"

Elwin frowned his brows.

"That's not glass my child! That's borosilicate glass!"

I gazed at the flask. I had absolutely no idea what this meant, and I didn't know if I should ask. An awkward silence settled between us. Arius had the same look on his face while looking at me. I found the situation quite funny and had to refrain from giggling. Elwin finally raised his eyes and caught our looks. He looked up and sighed.

"Don't they teach you kids anything in school anymore?"

Arius and I laughed a little.

"Borosilicate glass contains boron trioxide. This means it will not crack under extreme temperature changes like regular glass," Elwin explained. He immediately went to light a flame under the flask.

I watched intensely. We didn't have this kind of equipment at the pack's house. It wasn't something that we did. These kinds of experiments were new to me. I wanted to learn more.

"You're making it heat?"

Elwin nodded. "Yes, when the water boils, part of purified water will evaporate. At the same time, the essence of the flower will stay in the flask. When almost all the water will be gone, we'll be able to get rid of the leftover of the flower. At the bottom of the flask will be highly concentrated magic from the flower."

This was so interesting! I got closer to be able to watch all of it happening. The water wasn't boiling yet, but I wanted to witness it all.

"Well, that's very nice and all, but I need to get back to the Moon elves' lands," Arius stated.

I turned back to face him. "Really? You just came back from there."

He was grinning. "I know, but I left a very important person there."

I didn't dare jump to conclusions, but… "Is that so?" I asked teasingly.

He smirked. "It's a long story. I'll tell you about it another day."

I giggled. "Okay fine, I'll want to hear all of it!"

Seeing Arius happy like that was refreshing! I've seen him so sad, raging at himself and isolating himself. I was sincerely happy that he might have found love again. I was eager to hear everything about her.

I turned back to Elwin.

"How much time will this take?"

He pondered a little before answering, "probably up until tomorrow morning."

"Oh, I didn't think it would take that long."

Elwin looked at me. "Magic takes time. You must learn to be patient."

I sighed. I knew he was right. "I guess I'll get back to the library then."

"As you wish, my lady," he simply answered.

I exited the room and stumbled on my sister Kate.

"Hi Bianca! How are you?"

I smiled. I loved her so very dearly. She hugged me. I enjoyed her presence as I didn't see her a lot anymore, now that she was the Queen of the vampires.

"I'm doing fine, just making my way back to the library."

My sister smiled; she knew how I enjoyed the library. Kate had never been a bookworm; she was the more active sister. Growing up, I always had my nose in a book, letting myself drift into a wonderful world.

"I think I'll accompany you."

I nodded and grabbed her arm like we used to do when we were little.

"Really? What's the occasion?"

She laughed. "I want to read more books about vampires. I'm eager to know more about them. With the baby growing in my belly. Not really knowing if he'll be a werewolf, or a vampire, or a little bit of both. Maybe I can find more information in the library."

Hmm. That made so much sense. I guess this hybrid baby raised a lot of questions. Werewolves and vampires didn't usually associate themselves. Either way, I would be happy to have my sister by my side.

We walked together to the library, chatting about little things and our lives.

When we got back, I helped Kate find a few books she needed. She sat beside me and started reading.

The best part was that by casting multiple exits, I will be able to start invading the world at multiple spots at the same time. This was perfect! And still, there was only one entry into the underworld. I would make sure it was heavily guarded... only a fool would try to get in anyway.

When the main portal's seal will be broken, and I'll be able to travel myself to the world of the living. With all the living energy I'm draining from mortal creatures, I'm getting stronger and stronger by the minute. You hear that? You wretched wench! You will never stop me!

I sat straight into my chair, heart beating fast and sweating. It was that damned demon again. It seems he was opening portals into our world. This wasn't good! We weren't going fast enough; he was succeeding his plan way too fast.

Kate raised her eyes from her book and saw my face.

"Is everything okay?"

I shook my head. "No. It's Eurynomos. He's opening portals to our world."

Kate put a hand on her mouth as she gasped.

"I heard him say it! And he says he's draining energy from the living."

As I spoke those words, I came to realize something.

"Oh, my gosh! Kate! This is it!"

"What?"

"I'm sure of it! It's Eurynomos that's making father that sick! He's draining his living energy! I'm certain of it!"

I didn't know what to do with myself. As much as I hated being able to hear Eurynomos talking to me, this was a revelation! It answered so many questions. At the same time, I really needed to get this information to the others as soon as possible! This was valuable information for the war against the demon as well. I stood up, but I didn't know what to do first. My heart was hammering in my chest. Too many things at the same time. My mind didn't know what to do first.

I felt Kate's loving hands on my shoulders.

"Calm down, Sis. Let met help you. We're a team, remember?" she smiled.

She stopped for a moment and concentrated.

"I just called Damien through our mate bond; he's coming right away."

Right! The mate bond. How the hell didn't I think of that? I guess I was too overwhelmed. I concentrated on my sweet Steven that I loved so much. He was still with Zach and Lilith. I gave him all the information. He asked if I wanted him to come and comfort me, but I declined. I wanted him to prepare the army for battle. It was clear now that we would need to be prepared even faster than we anticipated.

A few seconds later, Damien emerged in the library with a serious face.

"I came as fast as I could," he said, out of breath. For a vampire to be out of breath, he must have hurried a lot. I wondered where he was, but tossed that question aside. That wasn't important right now. I explained everything to him again.

He listened to everything I had to say. When I was done talking, he asked, "okay, so to summarize. We know Eurynomos is draining living energy from your father. He's succeeding in his plan to break the seal on the main portal and planning to come here. In the meantime, he's spawning exits to get his army into this world."

I nodded. "Right! And he mentioned there's only one entry into the underworld, so it's likely to be heavily guarded."

"Right, that too…"

I thought back to a book I've read not too long ago. It talked of ancient demons and goddesses. It was said that the Moon Goddess was the one responsible for imprisoning Eurynomos centuries ago. Although an ancient pack oversaw guarding him, they failed at their task for an unknown reason. And so, it fell onto the shoulders of the Moon Goddess to once again fight back Eurynomos and seal him again.

Being the Moon Goddess's daughter, I knew the responsibility fell on my shoulders. But because of the curse bounding me to Eurynomos, it was impossible. Not only did I not have my full powers, but Eurynomos was aware of my every move and thoughts.

"I need to find a way to break this curse," I stated to Damien.

"I know. We also need to tell Will about the cause of your father's sickness. And the news about the demon's progress."

I nodded, but I didn't want to leave the library just yet. I wanted to read that ancient book again. I had the feeling it contained information on how to break the curse.

"I will go," Damien stated.

"No!" Kate shouted. "I need you here with me, with the baby. I don't want anything to happen to you."

Damien hugged her tenderly in his arms, leaving a hand on her still flat belly. He kissed her sweetly on the lips.

"I will be back. You will never be alone."

She shook her head. "But what if something happens to you? You're the vampire Lord! Your people need you."

"And you're their queen. They will be fine with you while I'm gone."

Damien took Kate's hand and put it in mine.

"You stay here with your sister, work as hard as you can to prepare for the war and find how to break the curse. You can always tell me everything that's happening through our mate bond. Should you need me, I will fly back. I promise."

I squeezed my sister's hand. As much as I understood, she didn't want her mate to leave, now especially since she was pregnant. He was right. It will give us an advantage to be able to use their mate bond to communicate between the pack's house and the castle.

"He's right Kate."

My sister nodded reluctantly. She turned to her lover. "Please stay safe."

He smirked. "Don't worry, I'll even bring Blake along."

He kissed her one last time, taking time to caress her cheeks. I could feel all the love he held for her. Then he gave me a brotherly hug.

Before leaving the room, he turned around and added, "I know I can count on you, my queen." He winked and left the room.

Chapter 9 (Will)

Witches

I couldn't sleep all night. My wolf was restless. I'm pretty sure she hasn't slept either. Even if she was in the furthest room of the house, all I could do was think of her, intoxicated by her scent. She had only been here for one night, but I came to a realization. I couldn't continue like that. I wasn't sure what I would do exactly. But I knew I needed to be with my mate. I couldn't lie to myself anymore.

Despite the fact I hadn't slept last night, I felt energized. I got the feeling it was because my mate was so close. My wolf wanted to see her at all costs.

I took a quick shower and got dressed in a nice pair of jeans and a simple t-shirt.

Jane was already in the kitchen when I got out of the shower. I would need to talk to her soon, but I still didn't know how I would manage that conversation. I took a quick glance to make sure I looked fine before going to join the others for breakfast. It was already late morning, but I couldn't care less about time right now.

I froze for a moment when I entered the kitchen. Leila was there. She looked tired, but she still was the most beautiful woman I had ever seen. My heart was racing, and my wolf wanted to come out. I reminded him, "soon." I couldn't go to her just yet. Things needed to be settled with Jane first. It wouldn't be fine to do things the other way around. Leila was staring at me. How I wish I could caress those beautiful cheeks of hers. I passed my hand in my hair and made way to grab a plate.

Jane motioned to come closer to me, but I changed the path as naturally as I could. I couldn't bear to kiss her right now, and I didn't want to talk to her in front of everyone. I knew this would hurt her. I knew she loved me. I used to think I could love her back, but I knew now it was impossible. She would be my best friend, like all these years, or at least, I hoped she would still be. But I couldn't keep her as a mate.

I sat down, and Jane sat beside me. She knew I had avoided her hug, but she was hiding it. Just as I started eating, the door to the pack's house opened. Damien and Blake rushed in.

"Will, we need to talk to you now!"

I stood up. For them to barge into the room like that, I knew something was going on. Before I even had the time to say anything, Ravynne asked, "does this concern Eurynomos"?

Damien and Blake froze and looked at me. Nobody would normally speak before the Alpha said it was fine. I also knew Ravynne was her own pack's leader. I nodded to Damien and Blake.

Damien finally spoke to her, "might I know who I'm speaking to?"

"I am Ravynne, chieftess of the Hands of Fate pack."

Damien frowned.

"The Hands of Fate pack? I have never heard of it."

"We are an ancient pack of werewolves and witches."

I twitched a brow at that word.

"Witches?" I asked.

Ravynne smiled, "yes, my Alpha. I thought you knew."

This was my first time hearing they were witches. I knew I didn't feel a wolf in Ravynne when they first came around. Same thing for Skye. The only one who had a wolf was Leila. I thought they were simply humans, like other members of my pack.

But to know they were witches raised questions. Although, I did see the color of their souls. Ravynne and Leila, their souls were pure white. I knew I could trust them. As for Skye, well… it was a little more complicated. I didn't quite know what to make of her soul. Most of the time, it's either white or black. But her soul was gray, and I didn't know what that meant. I preferred to stay cautious of her.

"Damien," I started. "These three women have come to ask our aid to fight Eurynomos. They claim a foul stench spreads on their lands. They believe it might be coming from a gate to the underworld."

Blake's eyes were wide open. Damien cursed.

"So, it seems it has begun."

"Let us speak here, since everyone is concerned anyway," I spoke.

The two vampires nodded.

"Your sister, Bianca, finally discovered the cause of the illness of your father."

I held my breath at those words. Finally, something encouraging. I had watched my father waste away for two years without being able to do anything about it.

"What is it? What can I do?"

"It's Eurynomos. He's draining energy life from your father."

I hit the table with my fist.

"Damn that demon! Is there nothing we can do?"

"Elwin is working on a concoction to try to heal him. Arius went to the Moon elves' lands to retrieve a very powerful flower in the hopes it will save him."

I bowed my head and breathed out. At least there was still hope.

"If I might," Ravynne interrupted. "Well, if you would allow me, Alpha Will. Leila and I could cast a protection spell on your father. I don't know if it would work on a curse that's already active, but it can't be worse."

I had nothing to lose at this point. "Alright, we will go, but first. Damien, what did you mean when you said it had begun?"

"Yes, Bianca also overheard the demon saying he had breached the main portal. Soon, when the seal is broken, he will be able to come to our world and claim all. But in the meantime, he began spawning portals everywhere for his army to start the invasion."

I was boiling at that revelation. So, the war had begun. We needed to defend ourselves.

"Then let's get to one of these portals, enter it, and deal with him at once!"

Damien shook his head. "We can't. Those are exit portals. There's only one entry into the underworld, and we are yet to find out where it is."

"Then what are we supposed to do?" I shouted.

"Bianca says we need to break her curse. As the daughter of the Moon goddess, she's the one supposed to take care of the demon."

At those words, Leila and Ravynne put their hands on their mouth. I sighed. I guess we had a lot to discuss.

"Let us eat. I will explain everything. We'll decide on a course of action after."

Damien and Blake weren't hungry. They took a seat and listened to the conversation, jumping in as needed. I explained to our guest about my sister, who was the daughter of the Moon goddess. We talked about her curse, and about my father. Ravynne explained to us how their ancestors were witches and werewolves. That some of the members of their pack were born both with witches' magic and a wolf, like Leila. Others were born with only one or the other, or even none, like Skye.

After eating, I went to my father's room with Leila and Ravynne. My heart was beating strong from being this close to her.

I opened the door to my father's room. My mother was by his side, as always. She had an inquisitive look when she saw the two women accompanying me.

I spoke, "mother, this is Ravynne and Leila. They are witches and will cast a protection spell on Father." Then I added, "if that is okay with you."

I might be the Alpha, but she was still my mother, and my father was her mate. She had the right to decide whatever she deemed best for her mate. It would be devastating if something were to happen to him. But she would be the one suffering the severing of the mate bond.

Sarah rose from her seat and came closer. She examined Ravynne and Leila, then came to me.

"It's okay, they can go ahead. I will go wait in the living room."

I nodded. "Damien is here if you want to see him."

She smiled; I knew she liked her son-in-law. Even more so now that she knew she would have a grandchild in a few months.

When my mother left, Ravynne and Leila went on each side of my father's bed. I stayed near the door to observe. I still couldn't get over the fact that Leila was a witch werewolf. I was so lucky to have such an amazing mate! I was curious to see the extent of her powers. I watched silently as they joined their hands together over my father's bed. They started reciting words I didn't understand. Soon, a white glow surrounded the bed. I could feel a warm wind blowing softly. Ravynne and Leila had closed their eyes, but were still joining hands, reciting the words even stronger. Their hairs were flowing with the wind. It was truly a magnificent sight.

The wind stopped at the same time they were done speaking the words. I couldn't get my eyes off of Leila. She opened her eyes and saw I was staring. I tried to look away, but it was too late. She smiled and I couldn't do anything other than to smile back, knowing she knew what I felt, because she felt it too. Although she didn't know what I intended to do, and I was eager to tell her.

Ravynne came towards me. "It is done."

I grabbed her hands in mine. "You have my gratitude, Ravynne."

She bowed her head slightly, and we exited the room.

When we joined the others back in the living room, they were all silent.

"What's going on?" I asked.

Blake turned towards me. "Bianca found out how to break her curse."

I was overjoyed with that news. "Really? How?"

Damien spoke, "She found it in an old book. It's a riddle. Listen. *Pour réparer un péché, commis il y a des centaines d'années. Une île flottante, au milieu d'une tempête foudroyante. L'épée sacrée devra être retrouvée. Et un trésor adoré devra être sacrifié.*"

I frowned. "What the hell is that?"

Damien shrugged his shoulders. "It's not English, for all that I know."

Leila added, "it's not Spanish either."

"Or Latin," added Blake.

Ravynne was thinking hard. "I think it's French, actually."

"French?" I repeated.

"Yes, our ancestors used to speak French. I've been taught some of it when I was a kid. Although it's been a while, I think what it says basically is: To undo a sin committed centuries ago. A floating island, in the middle of a thundering storm. A sacred sword must be found. And..." she put her hand to her mouth, not talking anymore.

"And what?" Damien asked.

"And a beloved treasure will have to be sacrificed..." she finished in a whisper.

"What does that mean?" I asked.

Everybody looked at me, but nobody had an answer.

I paced in the living room, playing the words in my head. This was stupid. We finally found a way to break the curse, but it was a riddle.

"If only we could find someone to help us, someone who had a great amount of knowledge," spoke Blake.

He was right. We've been thinking over and over again, but nobody could find anything. It was time to ask someone else for help. But who? Everyone at the castle must already be searching.

The only person I could think of was… Ayanna! Right! She lived for many centuries; she knew things nobody else could understand. Maybe she could help.

"Let's go see Ayanna, the Melian nymph Queen," I declared.

Blake laughed. "I have never seen a Melian nymph Queen in my whole life, but this sounds like the best idea anyone had so far."

"Then it's settled. I guess it means Leila, Ravynne, Skye, Damien, Blake and I will be leaving now."

"Perfect!" Damien exclaimed. Blake and he exited the pack's house. Ravynne and Skye were not far behind them.

Leila came closer to me. I immediately felt my heart beat faster. My wolf kept screaming: "mate."

She asked in a small voice, "are you sure about the vampires?"

"Damien and Blake? Of course! Why?"

"Are you sure they can be trusted?"

I smiled. Being a werewolf, of course, she was wary of vampires. But I had seen what they could do in battle. Damien saved my sister's life and even sacrificed his own to protect my family. He was my sister's mate and the father of their child.

"I would trust my life with them."

She seemed happy with my answer. Before she left, I asked, "are you sure about Skye?"

Leila frowned and crossed her hands on her chest.

"What do you mean? She's my best friend."

"Well… I have this gift. I see the color of people's soul. And well… Skye's soul is gray."

She now had an incredulous look on her face.

"You can see souls, and my best friend's soul is gray?"

"Please Leila, I know it sounds crazy, but can you just trust me on this?"

She sighed. I knew with the mate bond she would trust me. I mean her wolf must be practically begging for her to trust me… and probably begging to see my wolf and a lot of other stuff as well. I didn't even know how I managed to keep my wolf in check.

"Okay Will. But you must know, I also trust my best friend. She's like a sister to me. I've known her forever."

I nodded; I couldn't contradict her. She had known this girl all her life. And she knew me only for a few weeks, and well… I hadn't been the best for her so far. It was only natural she would trust her best friend.

I was getting distracted by my wolf. All I wanted to do right now was to grab her in my arms and kiss her. How I wish I could tell her yet, but I simply answered, "okay, you know her more than I do."

She seemed happy and started walking towards the door. Seeing I wasn't coming, she turned around and asked, "coming"?

"In a minute, I need to do something first."

She nodded and exited the house. I took a big breath. I knew what needed to be done. I wasn't even sure if I would find the right words. But now was the time to do it.

Leila's POV

The rays of the sun felt good on my skin as I exited the pack's house. I was feeling tired from not sleeping last night. I had to refrain from wandering the house at night. All I wanted to do was go and find him. But overall, I was managing fairly well this whole situation and was pretty proud of myself. I wondered how the next few days would go. I didn't really expect to go on a journey with him. But to my surprise, my wolf was feeling better now that I was closer to him. It did calm her to have her mate by her side, even though he had his Luna… How I loved seeing his smile earlier, after we cast a spell on his father. The way he was looking at me. If I didn't know he had a Luna, I could almost believe he liked me. For sure, he feels the mate bond, too. I guess we will have things to discuss if we get some time alone. For now, I decided to get those thoughts away and just enjoy the present.

"What do you think is taking him so long?" Skye asked.

I shrugged my shoulders, "whatever Alpha business he must have."

"Maybe he needs to kiss his Luna before leaving?" she teased. "Or maybe he needs to get her pregnant with pups before leaving."

A growl escaped my chest at that thought. It was a low growl, too low for humans to hear. My grandmother and Skye didn't hear it. But the vampires turned their heads my way. I ignored them.

"Would you stop it?" I shouted, annoyed.

"What? I can imagine them pretty good." she laughed and started doing mimics like she was kissing and hugging the air.

I rolled my eyes to the sky and sighed. Skye could be so immature at times! Nevertheless, I couldn't help to wonder if she was right. Would he be so arrogant as to make love to her before going? Knowing we were waiting for him? It did seem like he was opening up to me earlier. Did I dream it all? I felt so confused right now. My grandmother and Skye didn't know he was my mate. I knew Skye wasn't doing it on purpose. It was annoying me anyway and I couldn't help my wolf. She kept growling. The thought of my mate kissing this Luna, making love to her, was too much for me to bear.

Blake turned around and came closer to me to see if everything was okay. I didn't really want to speak to anyone about the reason my wolf was growling like that.

"Everything's okay?"

I heard Will's voice behind me, and my wolf calmed down immediately. My shoulders relaxed.

"Everything's fine," I answered. I turned to face him, but he had a stern face. I tried to read him, to understand what was going on, but I couldn't. I wondered what happened for him to be this way.

His mother came outside the house to see us off. I didn't see the Luna anywhere. Good, I didn't want to see her, anyway.

"Where does Ayanna live?" My grandmother asked.

"To the northeast," Will answered. "It will be better if we take the cars."

"I don't know how to drive," answered my grandmother.

Will raised an eyebrow at my grandmother's statement.

"We live secluded from the humans as much as we can. We like to be in harmony with the forest and rely on ourselves. I never needed to learn to drive a car," she explained.

"It's fine, I know how to drive," Will answered.

"So do I," added Damien.

"Leila, you can come with me," said Will. "The others can get into the gray car over there. It's got five seats."

I blushed at the thought of being alone with Will. My heart was racing just thinking about it. I know I probably shouldn't, I mean, he does have a Luna. But I had the feeling he did it on purpose to get the others in a second car and get me alone with him. My wolf was wagging her tail and I couldn't help but feel happy at that thought.

"There's no way I'm leaving my best friend alone," Skye shouted.

I grimaced at those words. Why did she have to say that? I know I didn't tell her Will was my mate, but couldn't she leave me alone for two minutes?

"That's okay. I don't mind going alone." I tried smiling, hoping she would get the hint.

Damien smirked behind her, but Skye didn't seem to understand. I never realized how dense she was before today.

"I'm coming, and that's the end of it!" said a very motivated Skye.

Before Will could even say anything, she was already sitting in the back of his car. She rolled the window down, shouting, "Coming?"

My grandma looked to the sky in exasperation. Damien and Blake were both laughing beside her. Will looked like he had a vein about to pop in his face. Despite the fact I would have preferred to be alone with him, I knew Skye only did that because she loved me.

I smiled at Will, trying to ease the tension.

"I guess we'll be three in the car."

Will relaxed and smiled a little. He was so handsome I thought I could melt away.

"At least sit up front, so I'm not alone while driving."

"Deal," I answered, grinning.

I turned to walk to the car. Will had already opened the door and was waiting for me to take place in the passenger's seat.

I didn't know how much time would take the ride, but I knew my wolf was already enjoying it. He gently put his hand on my back as I entered the car. I could feel the heat from his body and his enticing scent as I sat down.

Chapter 10 (Leila)

Ayanna

We drove for a few hours and Skye talked the whole time. Many times, I felt like Will would have liked to say something to me, but he couldn't. Even during the rare moments of silence, when Will tried to say something, Skye would start talking over him and cut him off. I could see frustration in his eyes. I couldn't stop myself from giggling when Will rolled his eyes at one of Skye's incredible stories.

At one point, my eyes met Will's eyes while he was looking my way. Somehow, I felt his stare was full of emotions, so many thoughts unsaid. I could feel how annoyed he was about the fact we weren't alone. He was also sad and scared of something. I really had the feeling he wished he could talk with me. I noticed his attitude was different from when I first met him, and I wondered what had changed. I still resented him for the way he spoke to me the first time we met. But my wolf wouldn't let me be angry at him as much as I wanted to. She was just happy to be with her mate and wanted to help him be happier.

I couldn't help myself. I grabbed his hand that was on the gearshift and gave him a squeeze. His frown immediately disappeared from his face. He was so handsome when he smiled.

I thought to myself. *"Don't worry, we'll talk later."* His eyes widened, and I knew he heard me. Just like the other day, when we were in our wolf form. But it wasn't supposed to be possible until the mate bond was stronger.

"How did you do that?" he asked out loud.

I tried to concentrate, to speak to him through my mind again, but I couldn't. As fast as it happened, it was gone. I shrugged my shoulders and answered out loud, "I have no idea."

"You have no idea how I did that?" Skye asked from behind. "Come on Leila! You were there! I guess I'll have to tell you all about it again!"

She thought we were talking about her. Not waiting for an answer, she went on with some weird explanation. Will raised his eyes to the sky and turned back his attention to the road ahead. I couldn't help myself and giggled. I looked outside, trying to ignore Skye. We were surrounded by cornfields on each side of the road. After a while, the cornfields made place to forest. Will parked the car in front of a big forest of ash trees. A few seconds later, the other car parked beside ours.

We came out of the car, and Skye was still rambling. Damien, Blake, and my grandmother came out of the other car. They were smiling and talking together.

"Next time, she's coming with you!" Will said to Damien and Blake, pointing to Skye.

They both laughed as Skye protested, "hey! Why? What did I do?"

He didn't answer and walked towards Damien and Blake. My grandmother came closer to me. She was smiling.

"Well, it looks like you had a lot of fun."

"Yes, I got to know Damien and Blake better. I had many questions on vampires, and they were happy to answer them."

"I'm happy to know you like them."

I really was! The fact that my grandmother trusted those vampires really meant that I could trust them. I mean, I know Will told me he would trust them with his life. I mean that's a lot… But my grandmother had raised me, so her opinion was even more important to me. Even if he was my mate.

"They had a lot of questions on witches too," she added.

Will spoke loud enough for everyone to hear, "alright! Let's make our way to the nymph's sacred grove."

He started walking into the woods, and we followed him. I couldn't help myself but to watch his ass as he walked. My wolf yearned for him so much!

The forest was beautiful. Even though a lot of leaves had already fallen, a few of them remained. The sun was already lowering in the sky. Fairies could be seen flying through the ferns and plants. For a moment, I wondered what fairies did when winter came. Did they hide in a small house? I didn't expect them to be here, considering it was already late fall. I thought they would have fled like the butterflies have.

Soon, we arrived at a very tall tree. I tried to see the top of it, but it seemed to be going on forever.

Will came by my side. "Impressive, right"?

I nodded.

"I was impressed too, the first time I came here. It's the Tree of Life," he explained.

"How can it be still full of flowers? It's Fall."

"The Tree of Life is always blooming," Will answered.

"You remembered," said a woman's voice I didn't recognize.

I turned around to see a tall woman standing. I had never seen someone like her and was amazed at what I was seeing. Instead of legs, it looked like her lower body was composed of tree roots. The roots came up to her torso. She looked human from the torso up. Roots and leaves made her a bikini. She had elf ears, but other than that, her face was one of a graceful woman. Her hair was long and composed of vines and lianas with flowers blooming in them.

Will slightly bowed his head.

"Ayanna, it's great to see you again."

She smiled. "As it is to see you. It seems you have brought quite a few friends."

Will laughed. "Yes, we seek your help."

"It's already getting dark. You will need to stay for the night. Follow me," she spoke.

We all followed her to a clearing in the woods. A few huts stood in the clearing. At the center of it was a fire pit. Damien and Blake were already preparing to light a fire. We all sat on wood trunks around the fire, along with Ayanna and a few other nymphs. Will had brought a lunch for everyone to share. We ate together while talking with Ayanna. She seemed to have a vast knowledge, so I hoped she would be able to help us with the riddle.

Damien recited the riddle to her. There was no need to translate it, as she spoke many languages and understood what it meant.

"A floating island in the middle of a thundering storm. A sacred sword." She pondered a little. "I think you need to go to the island of Delos."

"The island of Delos?" I repeated.

"Yes, according to the legends, the island is protected by the dragon Kholkikos. He guards the island by making it float high in the air with its breath and prevents anyone from entering by creating a permanent storm all over the island."

"That definitely sounds like a floating island with a thundering storm," stated Will.

"Why should we go there?" I asked.

"You should find the sacred grove of Ares on the island of Delos. I believe you will find the sacred sword in there."

Everybody sat silent, taking in what Ayanna had just told us. I wondered how we would manage to get to a floating island protected by a storm. This wouldn't be an easy task.

"We could fly up there," Blake proposed.

Will shook his head. "We all need to get there. Besides, passing through a storm produced by a dragon. It seems like a hard feat, even for a vampire."

Blake lowered his hands. "Damn, you're right."

"Why don't we call it quits for the night? We'll think of something tomorrow for sure," suggested Will. Everyone seemed to agree.

Blake proceeded to get some drinks out of a bag he brought. Damien and Blake drank some blood wine, while others preferred drinks that didn't involve blood. All around me, people were laughing. Skye had drunk a few beers and was now arguing with Blake that werewolves were better than vampires. Damien was talking about vampires' traditions with my grandmother. Will was talking with Ayanna. I was just happy, enjoying the fire, listening to everyone.

At one point, Ayanna came and asked to speak with my grandmother alone. The two of them went away in a hut.

I watched as Will stood up to pick up some firewood and pile it up by the fire. His muscles were showing through his shirt. My wolf was drooling, but I tried not to show it.

"He seems cute," said Skye, who was now sitting by my side.

My wolf growled lowly, but she didn't hear it, and everyone was too busy to notice.

"Not really," I lied.

Skye shrugged her shoulders. "Well; anyway he already has a Luna."

What the hell was her problem? I knew she was probably drunk, but still… She was annoying me so much right now! I had to fight against my wolf who wanted to slash out at her.

"Well, I'm off for the night," stated Damien, as he retired into his hut to sleep.

"Hey! Skye, come over here!" called Blake.

"Sure," she answered, smiling.

In an instant, she was off with Blake. My wolf felt better now that she was gone. I swear, for the past day or two, my best friend was annoying me. I didn't really understand where all of this came from.

"Is this seat taken?"

I recognized his voice right away, my heart fluttering in my chest. I looked around and realized that Blake and Skye were gone, leaving me alone with Will.

My heart skipped a beat when he sat beside me, close enough for our shoulders to touch. He was looking at me with a smile that could melt me away. I wanted to stay strong, remind myself how he treated me. But my heart was beating strong for him, and my wolf was yearning for him so bad.

Will's POV

My heart was beating so hard, I thought it would get out of my chest. I was so nervous to see how this would go. I had thrown everything away for her. I only hoped it would go smoothly. She was so pretty, even tonight under the fire's light.

I didn't really know how to start. I decided to do as I repeated it to myself so many times in my head.

"Leila, there's something I need to tell you."

She looked at me with her beautiful brown eyes. My hands were sweaty, my mouth felt dry.

"Listen, I wanted to tell you. Well, you know. About when we first met. What I'm trying to say is… I'm sorry."

I felt so stupid, it's like I couldn't form a straight sentence and all the words came out wrong. She just stayed there, not saying anything, staring at me.

I continued, "the way I talked to you. The way I acted with you. It wasn't right. And I'm really sorry."

I watched her, trying to read some kind of reaction from her. She looked surprise, but that's about all I could discern.

"Well, you already have a Luna anyway," she said coldly.

The way she said it, it hurt inside. I guess that's what I've been doing to her, so I totally deserved it. But I needed her to understand.

"Listen, I was only trying to protect myself. I was trying to stay true to my duties. The thing is… It was stupid. And besides, I don't have a Luna anymore."

Leila raised a brow. "Really? How's it so?"

"I broke up with her before we left, earlier today. I couldn't continue lying to myself. She will stay the Luna of the pack, at least for now. She's trustworthy to take decisions while I'm gone. But she's not my mate anymore. And we'll see what you want to do when we get back."

Leila frowned. "What makes you think I'll take her place?"

I couldn't believe her question. "You're my mate!"

"You didn't really act like one since we've met. You've been acting more like an asshole."

This hurt more than I had expected. I was so scared of losing her. I didn't know what I would do if she would reject me.

"I know… As I said, I'm sorry."

Leila crossed her arms on her chest. "Well, it's not because you're sorry that I'm going to sleep with you."

I sighed; this was not going as I had hoped.

"Please Leila, please just give me a chance to start a second time. I thought I needed to make all those choices because of my responsibilities as Alpha. I thought so many things… But I got it all wrong. And I realize that you're way more important than I thought. You're my mate, and I can't…"

I stopped; the words stuck in my throat. This was such an important and hard thing to admit. Leila was staring at me.

"Say it. I want to hear you say it."

I closed my eyes and took a big breath.

"Fine. I cannot live without you. I need you like the air I breathe. Being apart from you drives me crazy. Just give me a chance to prove I'm a worthy mate."

She smirked. Her beauty, when she smiled could rival the beauty of the stars in the sky.

"Hmm… We'll see." She winked. "You'd better be good."

I was relieved by her answer.

"Can we just look at the stars and talk?"

She nodded, and I finally allowed myself to get closer to her. I wrapped my arm around her shoulder, and she rested her head on my shoulder. I could feel her warm breath on my neck, giving me shivers.

We spoke for I don't know how much time. At one point, I was getting really tired. My eyes were dry. But I didn't want to get to sleep just yet. The fire was out for quite some time now, and the embers were barely giving any heat anymore. I just wanted this moment to last forever. My wolf was happy to finally hold his mate in his arms.

"Maybe we should sleep. We have a big day tomorrow," whispered Leila in my ear.

"Okay, you're right," I answered reluctantly.

She came closer to me, bringing her lips to mine. How I had longed for that kiss! I grabbed her hip with one arm, pulling her against me. Her lips parted as our tongues danced together. My heart was beating strongly, to be able to finally kiss the woman I loved. She tasted so good. I never wanted this to end. We eventually broke the kiss.

"I know it sounds crazy, but I love you so much, Leila."

She smiled. "It doesn't sound crazy."

"I guess this is goodnight?" I asked.

She laughed. "Yes, it is." She winked and proceeded to go into her hut.

I followed her with my eyes, making sure she got inside. Then I proceeded to my own hut. I was so tired from not sleeping the night before. I laid down and thought of her one last time. Remembering her enticing scent, the sweetness of her lips and how perfect she tasted. I already missed the heat of her body against mine. I remembered every part of her beautiful face, her soft skin, and the way her breath felt against my skin. Only then was I able to let slumber take me away.

I had such wonderful dreams last night. I could still remember his unique scent, the way he tasted. I dreamt of him all night. It took him a while, but maybe my wolf was right about him. I only hoped he stayed true to his word. I was afraid to be hurt again. But I was ready to give him a chance.

I went outside my hut and met Skye.

"Hey, you look like you're in a good mood this morning," she said, grinning.

I smiled back at her. "You're right. I had a wonderful night."

I stopped talking as a scent caught my nose. I turned my head to the side to see Will helping Ayanna and Ravynne with the breakfast. Damien tried to help as well, but ended up spilling a bucket of freshwater on Will. Everybody was laughing, except for Will, who was now soaked.

Skye and I couldn't help but to giggle as well, from afar.

Will removed his wet t-shirt, revealing his muscled chest. I almost stopped breathing at his sight. He was so perfect! My wolf was begging me to get to him. He looked up and saw me stare. He smirked at me, and I thought he was simply irresistible. I was just hoping I wasn't drooling too much. He turned around to get a dry t-shirt in his hut.

I was still trying to get this image of him out of my head when Skye exclaimed, "well, that man sure is something."

For a moment, I almost wanted to tell her to back off from my man. But then I remembered she didn't know he was my mate. I figured I was better off telling her.

"He sure is," I started. But before I even could continue, Skye interrupted me.

"Too bad he's not into you."

I crossed my arms over my chest. How dare she say that!

"What makes you think he isn't?" I asked. I was pretty much annoyed at her.

"Well, for starters, he already has a Luna."

"He doesn't anymore."

Skye looked at me, surprised. "How can you be so sure?"

"Because he told me, and he's my mate."

Skye's eyes widened, then she burst out laughing.

"Oh, God! Leila! You're the funniest! As if this could be true!"

I watched her in disbelief. How was it possible that my best friend wouldn't trust me? How could she laugh like that? I was feeling rather insulted and began to question everything I knew about her.

I was about to give her a piece of my thoughts when I was interrupted by a sexy scent coming from behind me.

"Hey ladies, care to join the rest of us for breakfast?"

I smiled and turned around to face Will, who was now wearing dry clothes. His muscles still hinted under his shirt. He was looking at me with a sexy smile.

"That depends. What's on the menu?" I asked, smirking. His smile widened, and he grabbed my hips, pulling me closer to him.

The next thing I knew, his lips were on mine. I put my hands on his shoulders as we kissed, pulling him even closer to me. It was only when I could feel the heat from his chest on me and his arms around me that my wolf was satisfied. Time seemed to stop as we kissed, and I hoped it would never start again.

When we finally stopped to breathe, I turned my head around to look at the face Skye was making, but she was already gone. Will was still holding me tight.

"I guess she went with the others," he spoke.

I couldn't care less about what she thought sincerely.

"I guess we should eat breakfast too," I suggested.

Will nodded, and we walked together, hand in hand, to go eat breakfast with the others.

Skye was indeed already sitting at the table beside my grandmother. Nobody said anything about Will and me. I guessed it was just so natural that nothing needed to be said. We sat together and started eating.

Everybody was talking lively, discussing how we were to go to a floating island surrounded by a storm. All kinds of ideas were given: airplane, helicopter. Blake even suggested a catapult, which we all laughed at. The problem was real. Going on this island sounded next to impossible.

"To get to an island protected by a dragon, you should find a dragon," stated Ayanna.

Everybody stopped talking. The idea sounded great except that…

"How are we going to find a dragon?" asked Will.

You could see that everybody was searching for an answer. Even Ayanna didn't seem to know where to find a dragon.

Suddenly, Damien rose from his seat. "I know!"

We all looked at him, eager to know.

"To the southeast of Will's pack. There's a waterfall. Hidden by that waterfall is the lair of Ladon; at least that's what the legends say."

I was truly surprised to learn that a dragon was that close to us.

"How do you know?" I asked.

"I went there with Kate one day. We didn't venture inside, but I know where it is. I can lead you there."

That sounded like the best idea we've had so far.

"You say it's a legend… Do you think it's true?" asked Blake.

"There's always some truth to legends," answered my grandmother.

We all nodded.

"Okay well, we should head there then," Will said out loud what everybody was thinking.

We finished eating in silence. Before we left, Ayanna asked to talk to Will alone. When they came back, she gave everyone her blessing. We made our way back to the cars and departed for the lair of the dragon.

Chapter 11 (Leila)

The Journey

I sat with Will in the car as we drove back to his pack. It was decided that once we got there, we would do the rest of the path on foot. I expected to be able to cuddle with him in the car, but he was silent. I wondered what Ayanna told him. He was different ever since she spoke to him. I know he was probably overthinking in his head, but couldn't see what it was about.

"Is everything okay?" I asked.

He looked at me like he just woke up from a dream or something.

"Yes, sorry, I had something on my mind."

He grabbed my hand and brought it to his mouth, placing a soft kiss on top.

"Care to share it with me?"

He turned his head for a second from the road to look at me, then concentrated back ahead.

"I was only thinking about what Ayanna told me. Regarding the rest of the riddle. A beloved treasure will have to be sacrificed… She wasn't clear on what the treasure was, but she said it will be the hardest part of our journey. She said that what needs to be done cannot be changed."

I was so focused on how to gain access to the island that I completely forgot about the rest of the riddle. I really wondered what it meant.

We were silent for the rest of the drive, both of us absorbed in our thoughts. We arrived at Will's pack. Before we left the car, Will turned to me.

"While we're in the pack's territory, I cannot kiss you or hold hands with you. I still haven't announced to everyone that Jane is not my mate anymore. I still need to know if you'll accept to be my Luna. So, for now, I can't let anyone know. I hope you understand."

His words hurt me; my wolf didn't like it. But I understood. His duties as Alpha of the pack forced him to have a Luna. I still haven't thought of if I wanted to be a Luna yet, but I think that when the time comes, I won't hesitate. I wished I could kiss him another time before we exit the car, but it was too late. Some pack members were already greeting us and waiting for us to get out of the car.

I sighed. "Yes, I understand." My voice was shaking, but I tried to hide it.

We exited the car. Will explained to his pack that he would be away for a while. In the meantime, Jane would be handling the pack's matters. My teeth gritted at that name. My wolf was letting me know she was well ready to be a Luna. But I couldn't say anything at the moment.

Luckily, we didn't stay long in Will's pack. Soon enough, we were already walking through the woods in the direction of the waterfall. Damien led the way, followed by Blake and my grandmother. Then there was Will and me and Skye. She was last and was continuously complaining that we were walking too fast.

"Can we stop for a minute?" she was asking.

"We just started walking," replied Damien.

A few meters further she would ask again, "now can we stop?"

To which Damien would reply, "at this speed, we won't make it before nightfall."

We kept walking slower, but it was always too fast for Skye. She kept tumbling on tree roots and wanted to hold my hand to avoid falling, but I was too preoccupied with staying close to Will to care for her. All the while we walked, he stayed silent and kept his distance from me. I wondered why. Terrible thoughts kept creeping into my head. What if going back to his pack reminded him that he loved Jane? I shook my head. This didn't make sense. I was his mate; he loved me. Even though the bond was not strong enough yet for us to speak to each other through our minds. He just had a lot to think about, I was sure of it.

At one point, Skye shouted, "I know a shortcut!"

We all stopped for a moment and looked at her with wide eyes.

Damien went to her. "*You...* know a shortcut?"

She nodded. "Yes, I do."

This sounded strange, especially since we were far from our own pack's territory, and even outside of Will's pack territory.

"Yes, we can pass through there. We'll get to the waterfall faster."

Nobody said a word. Everyone was evaluating whether to believe her or not. I have to say, even I didn't know what to think. It seemed to me that Damien's path looked better. Seeing that nobody was answering, Skye started crying.

"Come on, I'm part of this team, aren't I? I want to help too! I'm telling you there's a shortcut this way and we should take it."

I think that everyone took pity on her. Damien nodded. "It's true, you are part of the team. We'll take your shortcut."

We all started walking in the direction Skye had given us. Soon, the forest turned to a muddy marsh. Trees were growing in the muddy water. Fallen trees were layering the path. We had to be careful where we stepped, or we would stumble on the tree roots that were coming out, but we couldn't see. The ground was uneven. At some places, we had mud up to our hips. Soon, we slowed to a snail's pace.

"That's not really what I call a shortcut," muttered Will. Blake and Damien snickered, but Skye didn't hear them.

"I swear to you, we're almost there," she said happily.

Walking was very hard, and I regretted that we chose to follow her shortcut.

I stopped moving when I heard a hissing sound. I looked around, trying to find the source of the sound. Everyone else was searching, too.

Suddenly, I saw mud move and could recognize the pattern movement of a huge snake between Will and me. However, there seemed to be more than one. I could make out three snakes. I had never seen ones that big. It seemed to have no end. I didn't recall any specific kind of snakes living nearby either.

My mouth fell open when it raised itself on its body, letting its head come out of the mud. My heart was racing when I realized that it wasn't three snakes, but one hydra with three heads standing in front of us. I had heard of these creatures, but I had never seen one with my own eyes.

Its neck was very long and had a long crest coming down its back. The mud was still dripping down its neck, but I could see that somewhere down the back, the three necks merged into one very thick body. On each side of its heads were two fin-shaped ears. Its eyes were glowing white, without a pupil. Fish whiskers were coming down from its mouth filled with sharp teeth.

My jaw was clenched. I had no idea how we could defeat such a monster.

"We're so dead," stated Blake.

I looked at him. Damien screamed, "don't breathe! It has poisonous breath, and its blood is so virulent that even its scent is deadly."

Did he just say, 'don't breathe'? Yeah right! How were we supposed to do that? Blake was right, we were going to die here.

"You won't die, I swear to you." I heard in my mind. I looked up to Will, it was him. I knew it. He was smirking at me. I was happy to be able to hear him, although I really thought we were going to die by that creature.

The creature made a sound so high I had to cover my ears to protect myself.

"Leila, cast the protection spell, now!" my grandmother screamed.

She was right! With the protection bubble spell, we would be able to avoid its deadly scent. Without waiting, I closed my eyes and joined my hands together, trying to concentrate as much as I could. I chanted the words, *"tutela praesidium protection."* Again and again until I felt this warm energy flowing through me. I felt it shoot all around me. I opened my eyes back up when the energy stopped.

Will was looking at me with wide eyes. "Wow," was all that I've heard through our mate bond. A bubble barely visible encircled us. We could breathe without being scared of being poisoned.

I smiled at him. But our happiness was short-lived, as the creature shrieked, letting us know it wasn't done with us.

Blake charged at the creature, letting grow his nails and slashing at it.

"Don't drink its blood," reminded Damien. "It's poisonous."

Blake didn't answer anything, but I knew he heard him. Will quickly removed his clothes and let his wolf take control of him. I couldn't help but stare at his beauty. He turned his head to look at me. I saw his eyes flicker, letting me know his wolf wanted to see me. I let my wolf go out front and she responded to him. I could feel contentment from his wolf through our mate bond. He turned away and went to fight with Blake. Damien was already there, helping Blake.

I got my bow out and started shooting arrows at the beast. It was moving fast, but I still managed to get an arrow in one of its eyes.

The guys were scratching everywhere they could. Each head seemed to follow one of the guys. It was trying to spit poison at Will, but he was agile and avoided it. My heart fluttered to see him fight like that. At one point, Blake took a dagger out of a scabbard at his belt. He jumped in the air and slashed one of the heads. The creature shrieked in pain and the neck fell to the ground as the head did the same a little further. Purplish blood was dropping on the ground. We started to rejoice, but it was short-lived. The neck got back up. I heard a strange squishing sound as new flesh seemed to form. The neck separated itself into two halves, and two heads began to grow. In a matter of seconds, the creature now had four heads instead of three.

The guys stopped fighting for a moment.

"How do we kill it?" asked Blake.

"Don't you remember the old classes?" asked Damien.

"Do I look like I remember?" answered Blake.

"If you cut its head, two will grow back," stated Damien.

"Couldn't you have said that earlier?" asked Blake, grimacing.

"Didn't remember it earlier," said Damien, grinning.

"Then we kill it with magic!" I shouted.

"It could work," said Damien.

"You guys distract it, while Leila and I cast blaze on it," said my grandmother.

"You got it!" said Will through my mind.

I only hoped he wouldn't do something stupid and get himself killed. I looked around, but Skye was nowhere to be seen. Did she get eaten by that creature when I wasn't looking? I didn't have time to ponder. My grandmother grabbed my hands.

"Concentrate, Leila, we can do this."

I nodded to her and closed my eyes. All around us, I could hear the guys yelling at the creature to get his attention. I could hear them fight or get hit by the creature. It was hard to concentrate, but I knew I had to do it if I was to help them.

We started to recite the spell, "*flamma ignis caleo.*" This spell was an easy one. It was one of the first spells that I've learned. But this time, we needed to make it way bigger than we ever had.

Inside of me, I started to feel this warmth. It started to get so hot; it was burning all around my body, but I kept going on. Our lives and the ones of our friends, and of my lover, depended on it. We kept on and on until we couldn't bear it anymore.

At that point, we raised our hands to the sky, releasing the immense power we had amassed, sending it directly on the hydra.

I opened my eyes and was surprised to see the creature engulfed in flames, screaming and squirming on the muddy ground. The spell must have been much more powerful than I had thought. Suddenly I realized that Will, Damien and Blake must have been fighting the creature when we released the spell. Fear crept in me. I only hoped they didn't get caught in the flames. My heart was beating fast as I was searching for him. A hand soon fell on my shoulder, and I immediately relaxed.

"Good job," a low voice said.

Will was back in his human form, fully dressed.

I smiled at him. "Thanks."

"You guys are coming?"

We all turned to see Skye, who was up ahead, waiting for us.

"Where the hell have you been?" I asked. "We were fighting this creature. You weren't even there to help us."

I was furious at her. She should have been there, fighting with us. We could have been killed! All of that because of a stupid shortcut we took because of her!

"Were you? Oh! I'm sorry, I didn't hear anything," she said with a smile.

I rolled my eyes. Yeah, right, as if she didn't hear anything.

"Let's hurry. We can't be sure the creature is dead," spoke Will.

I nodded to him. We all made our way through the marsh.

Finally, a few feet further, we finally got back onto solid ground.

We were still a long way from the waterfall, and it was now clear that we shouldn't have taken Skye's shortcut. After a while, Skye was tired… again… I think everybody was tired of hearing her complain all the time. We decided to take a break in a small clearing.

Skye sat on a big rock. Will was talking with the others, planning our next steps.

I was watching him from afar. I wanted to spend more time with him. Yet, he seemed so busy with all his responsibilities that he barely had time for me. I was feeling sad about it and wasn't sure what to make out of it.

"Did you notice how cold Will is with you?" asked Skye.

"I don't know what you're talking about."

"Don't play fool, I know you noticed."

I sighed, "Listen, Skye. Will is probably just tired and preoccupied, like all of us."

She rolled her eyes. "I think that you're too needy of him. You stick with him like glue. The guy needs his freedom."

I watched her, pondering. Could she be right? Did Will need more space? Is this why he kept his distance from me?

Skye continued, "I think he needs to think you don't want him."

"What?" I frowned my brows. "Why the hell would I do that?"

She smirked. "Guys love to chase the woman that they love. He'll find you irresistible if he thinks you don't want him."

I admit I had a mixed feeling about all of this. I thought I knew Will at least a little. But right now, I was feeling lonely. I've already heard in the past that guys love to chase the woman they love. Maybe she was right? If I tried this, he might chase after me?

"You really think so?"

She nodded. "Yes, of course I do!"

I smiled at her. "Thanks, I guess it's worth a shot."

"That's what best friends are there for."

We continued talking together. After a few minutes, Blake came to see us. "Hey ladies, we're going."

We joined the others. I felt sad. I just wanted to spend some time with Will, but he was always so busy. I knew he was my mate. Weren't mates supposed to love each other? Love was so complicated. I wish things were easier than this.

"Hey, is everything okay?"

I jumped at Will's voice. I wanted to go see him, to hug him. I just wanted to kiss him and be in his arms. But I remembered the advice Skye gave me.

I kept my face as straight as I could and answered, "yes."

I didn't wait for a reply and made my way towards the others, letting Will stare at me with a questioning look on his face. I sure hoped this strategy of keeping my distance from him would pay off.

We just arrived back at the pack's house. I was excited! Elwin had finished the healing potion late last night. The content was crystal clear; you could have sworn it was only water. But I knew it wasn't.

I went directly to my father's room with Steven. We were both eager to try this potion. Elwin said the purification properties of the plant should be present in the potion, so I had high hopes. My mother was at my father's side, still reading one of her favorite werewolf romance books. I only hoped we managed to save my father, so she could live her own romance again. I could only imagine how she longed to be in my father's arms again. I knew I would find it horrible if something were to happen to my sweet Steven.

Just as those thoughts crossed my mind, he looked at me. His eyes were full of love, and I knew he understood what I was thinking about. He knew what my mother was living, because he felt the same when I was unconscious two years ago.

"I could never live without you my love," he whispered through my mind.

I understood just how much he loved me, and I loved him the same.

"Mom, we have a new remedy to try," I said softly to her.

She smiled and rose from her seat.

"Thanks, my dear. Please, go ahead."

Steven helped me get my father into a sitting position. He had lost so much weight that it was easy to lift him. The man I had known to be strong, the one who protected me as I grew up, was only barely living anymore and it hurt to see him like that.

Gently, I made him drink the potion. As the liquid passed from the vial into his mouth, it glowed with a white light. We set him back on the bed and waited to see if anything would happen.

My mother came closer. I wrapped my arm around her waist, and she leaned her head on my shoulder. I knew she needed the support. She's been locking herself up in this room for the past two years and I knew she felt lonely. She just couldn't get away from her mate. She needed to be there for him.

We waited a few minutes, but nothing happened. We were about to leave the room when my father's chest rose from the bed a little. He seemed to take a deep breath, as if he was breathing for the first time. Then he fell back on the bed.

We all wondered what had just happened. My mother checked his vital signs, and surely enough, he was breathing. I looked at his face and saw his complexion improve.

"I think this potion really helped him," my mother exclaimed. She was smiling for the first time in months, and it was great to see her like that.

"I know! This is great! Let's hope he continues to improve," I added.

Steven and I made our way out of the room. There were still things I needed to do. I had brought a book with me from the castle. An ancient book that spoke of an ancient wolf's pack. A pack that oversaw guarding Eurynomos. From the conversations Kate had with Damien through their mate bonds before we left the castle, it looked like this was Ravynne's pack. I was curious about her. Damien said it was a pack of witches and werewolves. I had never heard of them before. I went outside in the garden to read it, while Steven had some pack duties to complete.

Eurynomos's POV

Four portals were already open. The goblins wizards were working relentlessly to get as many opened as possible. In front of each portal stood a group of orcs. These creatures repelled me. They were dumb and grotesque and they smelled like rotten eggs. But they were strong and followed orders blindly. That's why I chose them to lead the destruction of the world of the living. When teamed up with a few goblins and their ingenious war machines, it made a great mix. What orcs lacked in intelligence; the goblins made up for.

The main portal was still sealed. I was annoyed at this stupid portal. One of my goblin wizards was still working day and night to get it opened. Sweat was covering his forehead, and he blacked out a few times, but I wouldn't allow him to stop. Screw him if he was to die. Another would take his place. His life was useless anyway. There could be no greater pride than to help me achieve world domination. And if he tried to leave, I would kill him either way. Those wretched creatures knew better than to try to fight against me. Ever since I took the throne from that arrogant Hades, they knew what I was capable of. That fool didn't deserve to rule the Underworld, anyway. He was sitting lazily on his ass. The guy had no ambitions. It was easy enough to overthrow him. Ever since that fight with the Moon Goddess, I've been wanting my revenge on her. She will pay the price for sealing me here. On that day, I swore to make her and her descendants pay.

Suddenly, I felt my life force leech spell weaken. I growled in anger. Who the hell dared to disrupt my plan? I looked around; the creatures were trembling in fear. But none of them had done anything to interrupt my leech spell. That meant someone outside of the underworld was the cause of it. I gritted my teeth. I knew without even checking who was the source of my problems. That wretched wench. I concentrated my thoughts into her mind. I hadn't been listening to her for a while.

I saw through her eyes. She was at her father's bed, and she was happy. What has that bitch done? How could she have managed that? No one was stronger than a demon! The link I had to her father was still there, but it was definitely weaker. I swear I will have that bitch's life. I'll torture her slowly and I'll make her watch as I kill everyone she loves. When she can't take it anymore, when she begs me to kill her, I'll let her suffer some more. Only when I've had enough that I would kill her, very slowly and painfully. I knew the Moon Goddess would surely watch her precious daughter all the while I torture her. I was already rejoicing *at that thought. Maybe she would even come to face me directly; now **that** would be something I was looking for.*

Anyway, it was irrelevant. Even if the bitch's father was free from my leech spell, it wouldn't matter. He was the first one, and he had such a strong life force! He was very useful when I needed it. But I was now draining the life force from enough people. He could die for all I cared.

I retired to my chambers. A succubus was waiting for me. I knew she would gladly do everything I ask of her in order to get more power. How I loved those lower demonic creatures. They were delicious and obedient.

"Do you need me to do something, master?"

She was waiting for me, her voluptuous curves alluring. I licked my lips while tracing the outlines of her breasts with my fingers, making her moan.

I sucked in a breath before answering, "be a good girl now, I need you to take it all in your mouth."

I brushed my fingers softly at her entrance, making her gasp. Her eyes glowed with desire as she whispered, "as you wish, master."

Chapter 12 (Arius)

Sweet nectar

The past two days had been wonderful. I was back at the Moon elves' lands with Elashor. She had introduced me to the other wardens and to their leader. The Moon elves' Queen is very gracious and wise. She told me there hasn't been another account of an elf and a vampire being mates. But she won't deny our love.

Now that we've got the Queen's blessing, Elashor was feeling way better about us. She's been openly presenting me to all her friends and her family. She doesn't leave my side and I couldn't be happier. At night, we would meet with the town's people at the center. They would get the guitars, lutes, and banjos out, and they would play, sing, and dance all evening. They sang of traditional songs, relating their ancestor's prowess. It was a pleasure to be able to make Elashor twirl and grab her in my arms as we dance the night away.

I was amazed at the quality of the fabric of the dresses and clothes the Moon elves wore. Although their designs were simple, you could feel the softness and resistance of the fabric. I took this opportunity to buy a few shirts for myself, as well as one for my brother and a dress for Kate. They would surely appreciate the gift.

Now that I've seen Elashor's town, it was my time to show her where I lived. I wanted to present her to everyone. I loved her with all my heart, and I was sure they would love her too. The trip home was enjoyable. I got to fly with Elashor in my arms. She didn't seem to be scared at all. Her sweet scent of lilac lingered on me as we arrived at the castle. She seemed impressed by the size of the castle.

"Welcome to my home, my love."
She examined the castle in awe.
"Wow… You weren't kidding when you said you were a prince."
I wrapped my arms around her hips from behind. She let herself rest against me. I couldn't help but to brush my lips against the soft skin of her neck, leaving kisses every time I touched her skin. She moaned, and I never wanted her to stop. We didn't have the chance to properly spend time alone together yet. I only hoped she would want me as much as I wanted her.

"Didn't you say you wanted to present me to your friends and family?" she asked.

She was right. I would have some time to ravish her body later. I also wanted to drink a glass of blood wine, as it's been a few days since I fed last time, and I didn't want to have a bloodlust in front of her.

"You're right, come, my princess."

She giggled at my last word.

"I'm no princess. I'm only a warden."

"You're wrong. You're my lover, and I'm a prince. Therefore, you are a princess."

I grabbed her hand gently and led her inside the castle.

"Welcome back, my prince," said the guards at the door.

I knew this princess thing was not something she was used to. She would need to get used to it fast, as everyone here will treat her as the princess she now was.

We walked right to the throne room. Kate was sitting on the Queen's throne, looking at some matters that needed her attention. The throne to her right was empty, as my brother was absent.

I bowed to her. Elashor looked at me and did the same.

"My Queen, Kate, my dear friend. May I take a little bit of your time?"

Kate raised her eyes from the letter she was reading and smiled.

"Arius, you silly! How many times have I told you? Enough with the formalities! You're a brother to me."

I laughed. I loved toying with her.

"You know I love to tease you."

She laughed and nodded.

I cleared my throat, taking a more serious look.

"There is someone I would like you to meet."

Kate's eyes landed on Elashor. She waited for me to speak again.

"Kate, meet Elashor. She's a warden from the Moon elves. And well, she's my mate."

"Your Majesty." Elashor bowed to Kate.

Kate's eyes widened.

"Oh Arius! That's wonderful! Your mate! How is it possible? I thought… Oh, never mind what I thought! This is great!"

She rose from the throne and came to greet us, unable to resist anymore.

"Oh please, stop with the formalities. We are family now."

Elashor looked at her, unsure of what she should do.

I hugged Kate in my arms. Seeing us hug, Elashor raised herself. She just had the time to stand that Kate was grabbing her hands and gave her a warm hug.

"I'm so happy to meet the woman who makes my brother happy," Kate said to Elashor. Elashor blushed a little, not really knowing what to answer.

"The pleasure is mine," was all she found to say.

I laughed and put my arm around Elashor's waist.

"I still didn't give her a tour of the castle. I think we'll be doing that now."

Kate nodded.

"Right, and I'll get back to my queen's duties… It can be so boring sometimes! Those letters just never stop!"

I laughed at her comment.

"Lucky that I'm only a prince then." I winked.

She smirked.

"Remember, you promised to help us when the baby will be born."

It's true, I did promise that I would take care of some of the kingdom's duties when the baby would be born, so that Kate and Damien could take some time alone to care for him.

"You're right, and I will keep my promise," I answered.

Elashor and I exited the throne room. When the door closed, Elashor whispered to me, "is she a vampire too? I mean… she's the Queen but, her skin is not white. She felt very warm to me."

"Right! I forgot to tell you! She's not a vampire, she's a werewolf."

"A werewolf?" Elashor asked, surprised. "I thought vampires and werewolves were at war?"

I laughed. "That's a very long story! Let's just say that my brother's mate is a werewolf, and well, peace has been declared between our kinds." Elashor smiled. "That's nice. I like the fact your kinds were able to put their grudges away."

"Yes, we also united to fight against the demon."

"The demon?"

"Yes, Eurynomos is threatening to come into our world. In fact, he already began spawning portals."

Elashor put her hand to her mouth.

I grabbed her hand gently. "Come, let me show you the castle. We can talk about demons later."

I brought her to the balcony on top of the courtyard. Down below were hundreds of humans, vampires, and werewolves. They were wearing armors and carried either a sword or a pike. Some of them had daggers or a flail. They were all following Lilith's orders. She was dressed in her full-plated armor. Everybody held her in respect, as they knew she was strong and powerful.

Together, they were training to face our common enemy, Eurynomos.

At the other side of the courtyard were rows of archers, aiming at targets.

A small group of elite fighters were trained by Zach. He had become way stronger since he became a vampire. He was the first werewolf-vampire, or at least, if there ever was another one, it was forgotten by history. Zach was already strong as a werewolf, but his powers decoupled when he learned to control his vampire's abilities. He was stronger and faster than any vampires or werewolves. He healed faster than any of us. He was able to control the minds of humans, use telekinesis, and control fire. I was happy he was on our side. He had begun fighting with a sword he was controlling with his mind. He loved to have both his hands free while fighting. His powers were even greater when it was a full moon night. That's why he was chosen as the leader to train our best elite fighters. Whether werewolf or vampire, he was able to help them decouple their powers and show them how to better control them.

Elashor was watching, speechless.

"If Eurynomos was to set foot on the Earth, we would need all the strength we can get to fight him. That's why we've been preparing day and night for the last two years."

She nodded. "I understand. You don't have elves training with you?"

I shook my head. "We didn't have contact with the elven race for a long time. The only ones we knew preferred to stay out of our problems."

"Oh, you must have met high elves, then. They don't like to mix with other races."

"Does that mean it's different for Moon elves?"

She smirked at me. "You should know more than anyone."

I grabbed her hand and pulled her to me. I buried my nose in the crook of her neck, smelling her sweet scent of lilac. She moaned as I licked her neck. She ran her finger through my hair, sending shivers down my spine.

I had wanted her for a while now. She was so graciously delicious, and I couldn't wait to taste her.

I told her voluptuously, "you smell better than the most exquisite flower. I wonder if you'll taste as good as you smell."

Elashor had a devilish smile on her face, making her look even more beautiful than she already was.

"I guess maybe you could show me your room next?" she asked with a wink.

I laughed lowly as I held her hand, pulling her gently with me as she giggled.

It didn't take us long to get to my room. I guess we were both eager. I could smell the scent of her arousal. I didn't know about her, but I've been longing for her for so long. I was already tight in my pants. We closed the door behind us. I pushed her against the door and kissed her passionately, intertwining my fingers with hers as I pinned her hands on the door above her head.

She whispered my name between moans. Her chest was rising and falling. Her nails were digging into my hands as she squeezed them.

I let go of her hands to start undoing her shirt. She started to roam my body with her hands. I couldn't hold a groan when she started licking my neck while rubbing herself on my cock.

That woman was driving me crazy. I finally removed her shirt, revealing her beautiful breasts. I took a moment to admire her beauty. Her elvish body was so small and graceful compared to mine. I wanted to make sure to worship every inch of her.

I brought her to the bed while taking off my shirt.

"I want to taste you so bad," I whispered.

She had a sexy smile. "Then do it."

I wanted to taste her in more than one way. But I didn't want to do it without her understanding clearly what I meant. We hadn't talked about that yet, and I needed to get that out before going further or I wouldn't be able to stop myself.

"I mean… you know that I'm a vampire, right?"

She giggled. "Of course I do."

She kissed me and managed to undo my pants at the same time. I removed my pants, revealing my enlarged member. She stared at me with desire in her eyes. I had a hard time focusing on what I wanted to say.

"What I meant is," I started as I got rid of the remaining of her clothes, admiring her smooth blueish skin. She was as beautiful as the stars, maybe even more.

"As a vampire, when we make love to our mates, we also drink their blood. It's the most intimate relation we can have. It's something that I yearn to do with you. But only if you'll allow me."

She raised her head from the bed. She grabbed my cock in her hand and started stroking it, sending me waves of pleasures. I couldn't hold my moans and she seemed to enjoy how she controlled me. Her eyes were still full of lust.

"Take me as you want. I want all of it."

I smirked at her answer. I didn't think she would accept that I drink her blood.

"I'll be gentle, I promise," I whispered between breaths.

She released my cock and grabbed my shoulders, bringing me to her. Our foreheads were touching.

"Don't be too gentle either." she winked.

I couldn't resist anymore. I brought the tip of my cock to her cunt. She was already dripping wet. I bit my lip, asking myself if I should ravish her right now or make her wait a little bit more. I gasped, as she thrusted her hips, sliding my cock into her. I loved how she took control. She was warm and tight around me. I started thrusting into her, adjusting myself to her cries. Waves of pleasure washed over me, as I felt connected to her more than ever before.

She had that spicy side that I was just discovering, as she begged me to go stronger again and again. God, I loved her! Many times, I felt I was on the edge, but I didn't want to stop yet. I liked to watch her writhe under me. My eyes kept going back to the soft skin of her neck. I knew my canines were already out in anticipation. I craved her so bad. I looked into her eyes, searching for her approval once again.

She screamed, "yes, do it!" in between moans.

I began licking her neck as I continued my thrusts. Soon, I felt her tighten even more. I just couldn't hold myself anymore. I bit her neck as gently as I could. She dug her nails into my back as I did, the tip of her nipples brushing against my chest. I started drinking her blood slowly. It was the sweetest thing I had ever tasted. She was my nectar, and I was getting drunk from her. I felt her heartbeat through my whole body, felt her thoughts and pleasure from inside out as I drank her blood. The feeling from our love making was getting so amplified from this connection. At one point, I started to feel her pulsing around me as she screamed my name in pleasure. I was overwhelmed by pleasure as I removed my teeth from her. I groaned hard as I came, still feeling her pulse around me.

I finally let myself rest on top of her, being careful not to crush her under my weight. She was looking at me with her appealing eyes.

"I love you so much, Arius."

I smiled.

"Elashor, if only you knew. Thinking of you keeps me awake. Dreaming of you keeps me asleep. Being with you keeps me alive."

I didn't know where this came from, but I just had to tell her how I felt. She blushed at my words.

"Please tell me you'll never leave me."

She kissed me softly, her tongue dancing with mine.

"I will never leave you, Arius. As long as you love me, I promise."

I lay down by her side, grabbing her in my arms, enjoying the warmth of her body. I needed to confess to her, "you have no idea. You saved me from a despair in which I was drowning for years." She didn't answer anything, just cuddled closer in my arms. I could feel her warm breath on my chest. It wasn't nightfall, but I couldn't resist falling into an afternoon nap in this perfect moment.

We were finally at the base of the waterfall. I knew the lair of the dragon was supposed to be hidden behind it. I thought that when we arrived at Ladon's lair, I would be nervous about meeting this dragon. I mean, who hadn't heard about the legend of Ladon? The dragon with a hundred heads! Or at least that's what they say. But sincerely, I couldn't care less about the dragon right now. All I could think about was Leila. I felt through our bond that something was wrong, but I didn't know what. She had cut herself off from me and I didn't understand why. My wolf was yearning for her. He wanted to go to his mate, to know what was wrong and to do whatever it took to make it better. But all the time we've been walking, she's been keeping her distance. Every time I tried to ask what's wrong, she replied that everything was fine. I knew it wasn't true. I only wished I could be alone with her and talk to her. I was her mate! I wanted to be there for her! If something was wrong, we could fix it together. This was so frustrating! Did I do something to make her mad? I didn't even know, and it tormented me to try to figure it out.

I joined Blake and Damien, who were searching for a way to climb up the waterfall, when I heard a scream.

We all turned around to find Skye on the floor, holding her ankle. Leila was by her side, looking at her leg. I rushed to them.

"What happened?"

Leila looked at me. All I wanted was to get lost in her eyes and forget about her friend.

"She fell on some rocks."

Leila looked at her friends and asked, "can you get up?"

Skye took Leila's hand and tried to get up. "I can't! I think I sprained my ankle."

I heard Damien sigh behind me. I tried to stay nice since Skye was my mate's friend.

"We haven't eaten yet, and we still need to get up this waterfall. Let's just take a break, maybe eat a little something."

"At this rate, we'll never get there!" Blake complained.

"We'll never get there if we're injured or starving," I added.

Blake was about to add something else, but Damien cut him off, "he's right."

Blake decided to stay silent. He wouldn't dare contradict his lord.

I started a fire on the shore of the Silent Lake. Skye was sitting near the fire. Damien was talking with Ravynne. The two of them looked like they had a lot of to talk about.

I overheard Ravynne speaking to him, "come! Let me show you the best herbs for healing. Let's see if we can get you to do any witchcraft."

He laughed. "You think I need more powers than the ones I already have as a vampire lord?"

"You never know when it can be useful to know witchcraft."

I thought it was amazing how quickly those two had become friends. It feels like Ravynne is treating Damien like his grandchild. Which is funny because when you thought about it, Damien was a powerful vampire lord and was more than two hundred years old. But I think he liked letting her play the role of the grandmother. I watched as they left the area to go look for herbs.

On the other side of the area, my beautiful Leila was there, speaking and laughing with Blake. My wolf was getting rather jealous. I had been wanting to talk with her for all the while we were traveling, and here she was, talking happily with him. I had to refrain myself from growling. I knew they would have heard me if I did, and it was ridiculous. I was her mate, not him. There was no reason for me to be jealous of him. I thought that I might as well go join them and see what they were talking about. But just as I was about to go, Leila got her bow out and followed Blake into the forest. They went so quickly; I didn't even have the time to tell them to wait. They were probably going on a hunt, catching something for a meal. With Leila being an excellent archer, they would catch something to eat for sure.

I couldn't go after them and leave Skye, who was wounded, all alone. I also needed to check the fire, so it didn't get out of hand. Defeated, I sat by Skye's side. I was watching the fire, throwing small rocks at it. I couldn't get the images of Leila and Blake laughing together out of my head. I was pretty upset.

"You know she loves him," said Skye.

What did she just say? I turned my head to look at her.

"You don't know what you're talking about," I replied harshly.

"Come on, you saw how close to him she was. You saw how she was laughing with him."

That girl had no idea what she was talking about. She was getting on my nerves a lot. I just wanted her to shut up.

"Stop it, you're just talking shit," I snarled.

"You know she's my best friend. She confessed her feelings for him."

I looked at her with incredulous eyes.

"What you're saying is impossible."

She shrugged her shoulders. "Hey, don't believe me if you don't want to. But I know what she told me. Why do you think she won't talk to you?"

I couldn't help to wonder if she could be right. Would that even be possible? She was my mate! How could she love another one? I tried to connect to her through our bond, and I couldn't. She shut herself off again. I needed her so much right now!

"Come on, she was even holding his arm as they went away."

My heart jumped in my chest at those words. Was she? I didn't remember! Was she holding his arm when she went away with him? That thought was eating me alive. I felt sick to my stomach. I didn't know what I would do if it was true. I mean, it would surely explain why she felt so cold earlier with me.

Skye got herself a little closer to me.

"You know… she might have decided to move on to someone else… But I'm still available."

My eyes widened as I looked at her. Please tell me I didn't hear right what she just said! But surely, she had that smile on her face, like she was trying to flirt with me. It was just getting me sicker. I was so shocked that I couldn't move. How could she even imagine that I could be interested in her? My heart belonged to Leila and no one else.

One second, I was lost in my thoughts, the other one, Skye's lips were on mine. I almost gagged at her touch. She wasn't the one I wanted to be kissing.

I heard a woman's voice from afar, "how dare you!"

I pushed Skye away, almost making her fall to the ground, and turned my head just in time to see my sweet Leila running away.

I stood to go after her, shouting her name, "Leila!"

Skye stopped me, grabbing my arm.

"You don't need her, anyway."

I frowned at her and snatched her hand from my arm. I was so pissed at her right now. But there were more urgent matters. I needed to go after my mate.

I tried to see where she ran away, but she was already gone. Her wolf was fast. I wasn't sure if she had turned to her wolf form or if she stayed in her human form. But I could smell her scent perfectly, her sweet scent that I yearned. I would be able to find her for sure. I needed to talk to her. We could set things straight; I knew we could. At least now I knew she didn't love Blake, or she wouldn't have reacted that way. I didn't even know how I could have thought she loved him. Without wasting time, I ran after her, following her scent through the forest.

Chapter 13 (Leila)

First blood

I ran through the woods. Tears were falling down my cheeks. I couldn't shake that pain and sadness I was feeling. Not only did I get betrayed by my best friend, whom I've known for my whole life, but I was betrayed by my mate. My wolf was hurting. She was howling in my chest. I just ran, without looking where I was going. I felt a sharp pain in my chest and my vision was blurred from crying. I just wanted to run as fast as I could, as far away as I could. My legs hurt, but it was nothing compared to the ache I was feeling in my heart. I just kept going on.

I wasn't sure where I was anymore, but I couldn't care less. I would keep going until my body couldn't keep up anymore. Only then would I let myself drown in sorrow.

Suddenly, I heard a loud roar. I stopped moving and looked in the direction of the growl. My mouth fell open. I couldn't believe what I was seeing. There, only a few feet from me, stood a chimera. I had never seen such a creature, only heard of them. It was said to be an offspring of Typhon and Echidna. I always thought they were extinct.

The creature was at least ten feet tall. Its body was massive! Its lion head was roaring aggressively at me, its jaws open, letting me see its sharp teeth. On the back of the creature was the head of the goat. Although it didn't have sharp teeth, it was breathing fire. I guess it explained the burned down trees surrounding me. In my rush to run away, I didn't even notice them. At the back of the creature was a long, scaly tail that ended with a snake's head. I had heard that its bite was highly poisonous. Its front paws also had huge, strong nails.

The creature was trying to attack me with all its heads at the same time. I was barely able to avoid its paws while dodging the fire it was breathing. Fear had replaced the sadness I was feeling earlier. My heart was hammering in my chest as I tried to figure out how I could defeat this beast. It was clear to me that I didn't stand a chance. It would catch me easily if I tried to run away. It was way stronger than me.

I tried shooting arrows at it, but the creature's skin seemed too thick for them to pierce through it. And arrows do poorly against fire.

"Aim for the eyes!"

I turned my head to see Will running towards the beast. I had no idea how he found me this fast, but I was glad he was there.

I did as he said and shot arrows in the eyes of the creature. It was moving fast, and it was hard to aim directly at it. It had three heads, so I wasn't sure exactly which head to target either! I decided that the lion's head was probably the closest to me and the most aggressive one. It also seemed likely that it was probably the one controlling the body.

Will had grown his nails and was fighting bare hands with the beast. He succeeded in slashing a wound open in the neck of the beast. It growled in pain and charged back with even more force. I finally managed to get an arrow stuck into one of its lion's head. The creature howled and stopped attacking for a moment. It was trying to get its eye free from the arrow.

"Quick! Come!" Will shouted at me.

He was right. The creature's attention was diverted. Now was the time to flee. I followed Will and ran in the forest with him, further from the burned trees. We continued running until we couldn't hear the chimera anymore, until we came to a clearing and were sure the creature wasn't following us. Only then did we allow ourselves to catch our breath a little bit. Only then did I realize that I now had to face what had happened earlier. Will was there… My mate. He saved me… But he betrayed me… I didn't know if I should feel happy or sad. My heart was lost, as well as was my wolf.

I was feasting on the sweet flesh of a dead goblin. It had died earlier, from exhaustion. His blood was still warm. I didn't need to cook the flesh. I loved to tear it apart and eat it raw, letting the blood fill my mouth before swallowing. It added a flavor to the flesh I couldn't quite describe. One of my favorite flavors, by far. My minions watched in horror as I devoured one of them. I couldn't care less about what they thought.

Suddenly, I heard cries coming from the other side of the Underworld.
I watched as two orc barbarians were bringing a young angel to me. She was screaming and trying to get herself free from their grasp, but wasn't strong enough, as she was so young.
I laughed and left my meal to go greet her. This was a rare sight! Such power. I knew I needed her.

"Hey there little girl, come inside... I've got some sweet things." I told her, as nicely as a demon can get.
One of my goblins immediately brought a cup of blood to make her drink. I came closer to her, to... persuade her. She was resisting, turning her head away, sealing her lips from the cup. I was

getting frustrated at her. She even had the impudence of spitting back the blood at my face.

"You foul demon! I will never side with you! Let me go already!"

I laughed lowly. "Such courageous words for someone in such a bad position."

All the while she continued fighting, trying to break free from the orcs holding her.

"Now, now, my child. There's no need to fight. I don't mind if you take what's yours, as long as you give me mine."

I knew I wanted her powers to be mine. She might have been young, a little more than eighteen years old. I also knew angels were incredibly strong. Those wretched creatures seemed to have decided to make war on my kind. I never really understood why. You rarely got your hands on an angel, so this was a rare occasion that I couldn't miss.

"There is nothing I want from you, filthy demon!"

She was getting on my nerves with her insults. I didn't want to kill her. If I couldn't get her the nice way, it would have to be the other way around.

"You want to see how mean I can be? You want it the hard way? So be it! One way or another, I'll have my way with you!"

She began fighting even more.

"Bring her to a cell. Lock her tight! Don't let her escape, or you know what will happen if you do," I threatened the orcs. They trembled in fear but shook their heads.

I watched them go away, dragging the angel to a cell. Her screams were echoing on the walls, sweet music to my ears. A few feathers fell to the floor while she fought to get free. She was wearing a small tight dress, revealing slender legs. I didn't want to admit the thoughts that came to my mind while watching her beautiful ass.

"You filthy demon! Don't you dare touch her!"
I laughed as I heard the wench talking to me through her curse. Knowing how disgusted she was by my actions only made it funnier.

I went to look at the magical sphere that was floating near the portal. Inside it was a blinding white small piece of soul, shining so brightly it was almost blinding. How I wanted to crush that piece of soul, swallow it all with darkness. I had tried so many times but couldn't. That wretched bitch was too strong. The Moon Goddess's powers were too strong within her, but she didn't even know it. If she was to gain back her soul completely, she would be a threat to my domination plan. But it was unthinkable for them to succeed.

I watched further; dozens of exit gates had already been opened. Even though they were small, my army had already begun spawning into the world of the livings, one by one. The invasion had already begun. It was only a matter of time before I was free from the underworld.

"Do you hear that? Moon Goddess's daughter, my dearest enemy. It's only a matter of time before I crush and destroy you!"

Bianca's POV

It was evening, and I was back at the castle. The full moon was shining in the sky. I was on the highest balcony with Kate. Lookups had warned us earlier that an army of orcs, centaurs, harpies and goblins were seen raiding the nearest town. Nobody knew where they came from. They just seemed to have appeared. But I knew they were coming from Eurynomos's gates.

Kate had sent some troops to take care of them. The demon's army was now at the castle's gates, trying to get inside. There were at least fifty of them. I wondered how it was possible that there could be that many already. I knew there would be only more if we didn't manage to close the doors.

The orcs were hideous. They wore hide armors with spiked shields. They wielded axes and flails. They didn't look like they were very smart and didn't seem to have a strategy. They just ran and tried to hit whatever they could. The goblins were the ones I feared more. They had strange flying machines and threw homemade bombs at us. They were uniting their efforts against a common foe, making them more dangerous than the orcs.

Centaurs were waiting for the castle's gates to break open and harpies were trying to grab archers to make them fall to the ground.

Lucky for us, our army far outnumbered them. All were fighting bravely to kill the demon's army. In the midst of the fight, I saw an orc being projected high in the air. When I looked down, I saw two huge white wolves fighting against the orcs. One of them was my sweet Steven. How I loved his wolf. But I didn't know the other one. White wolves were so rare.

I asked Kate, "do you know who this is? I never met him before."

She shook her head. "Barely. He came by a few days ago. His name is Cain. He says he's searching for a cure to his lover's curse."

I watched as the white wolf fought orcs by my mate's side. They were teaming up, decimating the enemy's army. I looked closely and noticed that Cain seemed to be sneezing.

"Is he… sneezing?"

Kate giggled. "I was told he was allergic to wolves."

My eyes opened wide. She continued with her explanations, "he took some allergies pills, but there are so many wolves in the fight. I guess it's not enough to prevent him from sneezing."

The situation was funny, but I tried not to laugh. These men, werewolves, and vampires were fighting for us. Now was not the time to make fun of this great fighter.

Kate added, "he said he would stick with us until Monday."

"Monday?"

She nodded. "He said something about a support group. Coffee and biscuits."

"This is kind of weird… I've never heard of support groups nearby."

"It's supposed to be run by a vampire."

"A vampire? Sounds like they should rather serve blood and biscuits."

Kate laughed. "I guess Damien would like it then, not that he needs support about anything. But he loves to have a good glass of blood, once in a while."

I smiled at my sister. I wondered what it felt like to be mated to a vampire. I would never admit how curious I was. My mate was a werewolf, and I loved him dearly. But I wondered, just a little bit, how it would be if he was a vampire.

On the lower balconies were archers. I could recognize Elashor. She was a dual sword wielder, but was also a skilled archer. Her skin seemed to glow under the moonlight. She was aiming dead on, killing off goblins and harpies, preventing them from coming too close to the castle. The harpies screeched high when hit by the arrows, and the goblin's flying machines would crash on the ground as their pilots died. On the ground, Arius was slashing and biting through enemies. At his side was Lilith, fighting with a sword. She was strong, and she cut through enemies like a hot knife through butter. The one who was killing the most was Zach. He fought with both his hands, nails sharp and teeth out. He also had his favorite sword levitating at his side, stabbing enemies. His powers were decoupled by the full moon. He was so fast; I had a hard time following him. I could only see the corpses piling up near him.

Near Zach was a very tall man with pale blue skin. He was covered with black inked tribal tattoos and had dark crimson eyes. His muscles were showing through his clothes. A kind of dark aura seemed to emanate from him, making him look very mysterious. He seemed to have a special sword that was made of a very strong metal. I had never seen anything like it in my life. He shouted while slashing through the demon's army, "I'm coming Syra, wait for me!"

I turned to Kate. "Who the hell is that? I never saw anyone like that."

She shrugged her shoulders. "His name is Zarek. He showed up a few weeks ago. He said something about keeping the Soul Realm from crumbling. Something related to the blood of the lion. Zach saw the potential in him, and although he was already highly trained, he decided to help him decouple his powers even more."

I watched in awe as the swordsman killed the orcs, blood gushing out everywhere. His face was splattered by the enemy's blood, but he didn't care. His goal kept him fighting. I wondered who this Syra was.

I watched the fighters. This wave wasn't a threat to us. We could relax, knowing they would be dealt with soon enough. I only hoped there wouldn't be too many waves.

I went back inside the castle with my sister. We stumbled upon a vampire walking with two female vampires at his side. He was walking bare chest, with a pair of jeans, showing his muscles. I couldn't help looking at this fine piece of meat, noticing he had a few small moles on his stomach. He smirked when he saw me stare, his red eyes lighting up with desire. I could notice the bulge in his pants, even from the distance. I giggled at myself when I suddenly started and wondered what he looked like without pants.

The two women at his side were staring at me. One of them had brown hair with highlights.

Her eyes were also red with gold flecks. Her fangs were out, and she was wearing a black corset and tight pants. The other woman had long brown hair with deep red eyes. She was wearing a tight red dress and high heels.

"Jake, we weren't done yet," they complained.

"Don't worry ladies, the more the merrier."

He came our way. "Would you care to join our little party?"

He had a sexy look in his eyes, his fangs showing a little bit while he smiled at me and my sister.

"How dare you talk like that to your Queen!" Kate shouted, angered.

Jake slightly bowed. "My apologies, my queen."

Kate held her head high, but seemed satisfied with his apology.

"You should watch how you present yourself to your Queen. If the Lord was here, he wouldn't appreciate it very much."

Jake had a devilish smile on his face. "But he isn't here, is he?"

I loved Steven so much, but this vampire was very tempting. Although I would never go to him, there was something sinful about him that attracted me like a magnet. He raised a brow, as if reading my thoughts.

"I can remove my pants if it's what's bothering you."

I froze. As much as I would have liked to see, I answered, "you should keep them on."

He laughed lowly, licking his lips. He knew very well the effect he had on me, and was enjoying it very much. The two women by his side seemed impatient, trying to get their hands on his body. The one with the corset licked his neck, biting his earlobe slightly, earning a slight groan from him.

"Instead of walking bare chest, you should put on an armor and fight outside, with the others," Kate spoke.

He bowed and winked. "Whatever my Queen wishes, I shall grant her. However, I do believe I have unfinished business to attend to first."

He turned back, grabbing the two vampires by the waist. He pulled the one with the corset in his arms, kissing her, sharing one breath, earning a moan from her. The other woman started to get impatient, trying to get attention from him as well. He only turned his head our way, adding, "have a great evening, my ladies. Do tell me if you change your mind."

He went to his room with the two women.

Kate sighed when he disappeared.

"The nerves this guy has, in front of his queen!"

I laughed. "Can't say I didn't enjoy seeing his sexy ass, though."

Kate burst out laughing at my comment.

"He was sexy indeed. Although I don't think Damien would appreciate to have a half-naked vampire walking around in the castle."

I nodded. "Of course! But my eyes appreciated the view, so I'm happy Damien isn't there to make him dress up."

Kate put her hand on her mouth, giggling.

"Of course you can watch. But you can't touch." She winked.

Chapter 14 (Leila)

True love

I was in the clearing of the forest with Will. We couldn't hear the creature anymore, which was a good sign. However, now that I wasn't running away from a creature, the image of Will kissing Skye was vivid in my mind. The pain was still sharp in my heart, making me sick to the stomach. He was staring at me; I could feel him hesitating as well. I was angry and sad at the same time.

"Why did you come and find me?" I asked, "you seemed to be getting along nicely with Skye."

"Please Leila, just listen to me."

He tried to come closer to me, but I took a step back.

"Whatever you have to say, now would be a good time to say it."

"Leila, believe me, I don't like Skye."

I snorted at him. "Yeah right, it sure didn't look that way."

He brought his hands to his face. "I know, but you don't understand! She forced me!"

"She what?"

I raised my brow. I had trouble believing this girl, born without a wolf or magic, could force an Alpha werewolf to do anything.

Will continued, "she was just saying how you were distant to me, and how you were close to Blake, and that… you loved him. She even said you confessed your feelings to her!"

I was taken aback by what he said. Did Skye really tell him I loved Blake?

Will kept going on, "I was thinking about what she had said. It hurt so much to think it could be true. It broke my heart. I was lost in my thoughts when, without warning, she started flirting with me and kissed me. Please believe me, Leila, you're the only one for me. You're my mate, my everything. I need you."

I watched this strong Alpha fall to his knees, his face in his hands, tears falling down his cheeks, begging for me to believe him.

I would never have thought to see him this way. I could feel how genuine he was, pouring his heart out for me. All the anger I had towards him was gone. My wolf wanted to care for him. I fell to the ground and took him in my arms. I immediately felt relief at his touch.

He looked into my eyes. "Please tell me you don't love Blake."

This was the silliest thing I had ever heard, and I started to feel anger in my chest at Skye who had set us up. I never thought my best friend could have done that.

"Of course, I don't. Oh, I can't believe she would say something like this."

"I don't care about her. The only thing I care about is that you don't love him."

"Will, I could never love anyone but you. If only you knew what Skye told me. She tried to say you were distant to me and that I needed to keep my distances from you."

He frowned. "I told you her soul was gray. She can't be trusted."

Skye had been my friend for so long. I thought I knew her. I had this bitter taste in my mouth.

I nodded to him. "You're right, you did tell me, but I didn't believe you… I guess the color of her soul says more about her than I thought."

I took a deep breath and added, "that bitch, I'm going to give her a piece of my mind when we get back."

I was rumbling everything I would say to her in my mind, getting angrier by the minute. The only thing I wanted right now was to spit out everything I had to say to her face. Our friendship was over for all that I cared. I didn't even know how I would look at her without ripping her face out.

Will's kiss made all the anger I was feeling disappear.

"Let's not focus on her right now. I want to focus on *us*."

I nodded to him while he gently caressed my cheek with his hand. His touch was giving me shivers. I never wanted to be away from him.

"You're right. She's not worth our energy. Let's just be careful when we're around her," I agreed.

"So…" started Will, "where does that leave us? Do you still love me?"

My wolf was begging me to melt into his arms.

"I love you so much, Will, you don't even know. I don't even want to sleep at night, as being with you is better than any dream I could ever have."

Will hugged me tightly in his arms. I was immediately surrounded by his sweet scent, my heart beating strong.

"Oh, my sweet Leila, I don't even know how I could have thought you didn't love me."

He stroked my cheek gently with his hand, butterflies making their way in my stomach. I kissed him, never having enough of him.

"I was so scared of losing you," Will whispered in between kisses.

My wolf was yearning for him so bad. I couldn't fool myself; I loved this man more than anything. My body was reacting to Will's touch. I wanted to be his. I wanted to be his Luna. I wanted to be with him forever.

"Will," I asked. "Take me, make me yours."

His eyes flickered, and I knew his wolf had heard me.

"Are you sure about this? There's no going back."

He was so close; I could basically feel the restlessness of his wolf inside of him. I knew he wanted this as much as I did.

"Yes, please, I can't take being away from you…"

Will looked at me. He seemed to hesitate. Once you're marked, it can't be undone. But I wanted him more than I ever wanted anything.

"Don't be shy, I won't bite," I added with a wink.

A low sound came from within him. That's all the encouragement he needed. His wolf was calling to mine. My wolf was wagging her tail, screaming to get out.

Will's laugh was irresistible. "We should get them together before they get out by themselves."

I smiled at him. He was right. It was about time I let my wolf out.

I watched Will remove his shirt slowly, revealing his muscled chest. He was so irresistible; I was already wet from anticipation. He smirked at the scent of my arousal. I started to undo my shirt, but Will interrupted me, "here, let me help you."

He started to roam my body with his hands, making goosebumps appear everywhere he touched. My nipples were hard and all I could think about was that I wanted to remove this bra that was annoying me.

"Get that out of the way before I rip it off," I thought.

He smirked and answered through my mind, "gladly."

I smiled; I was happy to see our mate bond was restored. Once the mating will be complete, I know it will only strengthen.

Will proceeded to undo my bra, reaching under my shirt, and sliding it through the sleeve.
I left out a breath when my breasts were finally free, the fabric of my shirt brushing against my hardened nipples.

Will took the time to admire the bumps they were making through my shirt, biting them slightly through the fabric, making me moan.

I started to kiss him while grabbing his perfect ass with my hands. His bulge was pressing against me, making me even more wet than I already was.

I undid his pants, finally getting him free. I couldn't resist but to lick him, slowly taking him in my mouth. Hearing him groan only made me hungrier for him.

"Oh Leila, baby. Stop or I won't be able to hold back." He was breathing heavily, and I could feel his cock almost throbbing in my mouth. I loved to control him like that, but I didn't want it to end now. I decided to let him free and got back to kissing his lips instead.

Will almost tore apart my clothes as much as he was in a hurry to remove them. He lay me gently on the ground while kissing. His fingers soon started to thrust into me, making me moan. I couldn't help but to rock my hips at his fingers. He liked to play, switching from my cunt to my clit, then going back in. He continued, for I don't know how much time. All I knew is that at one point, I arched my back in pleasure as I came hard from his touch, screaming and moaning.

"Good girl," he stated with desire in the eyes. He licked his fingers, then proceeded to kiss me, the taste of my wetness lingering in his mouth.

My body was reacting to his every touch. He was taking pleasure in watching me writhe. I gasped as he penetrated me. His cock fit me perfectly, touching just the right parts of me. I could feel myself getting tighter around him with every push.

He started licking my neck, giving me shivers. I felt his canines pierce the skin where the shoulder meets the neck. The pain only lasted an instant and was immediately replaced by an intense pleasure. He began thrusting harder and harder inside me, my walls closing around him. I dig my nails into his back as I came another time. Almost immediately after, he came hard too, pulsing inside of me while removing his teeth from my neck.

We stayed in each other's arms for a few minutes, recovering.

"I can't believe how perfect you are. I will always treasure you with all of my love."

His words were sincere, and I felt the same. I could feel my wolf pulling, begging me to let her free. I looked at his eyes. I didn't need to say anything. He understood, he felt the same.

I let my wolf take control of me. When I was fully changed, I was facing Will's beautiful gray wolf. I couldn't believe how strong and beautiful his wolf was.

"Wow," I whispered through our mate bond.

"You should see yourself," Will answered in my head.

His scent was just driving me crazy. I went ahead and rubbed my head against his, mixing our scents. I could feel how happy my wolf was to finally be able to be one with her mate. She had been longing for this for so long.

We took a run together through the woods, letting our wolves bond even more. After a while, we returned to our clothes. We changed back to our human form, and kissed once again before getting dressed. I could never have enough of him.

We walked back to the others hand in hand, never wanting to break our touch. I was happy to know the mark on my neck would remain there forever, showing everyone I was his mate. The fact I was now a Luna didn't even cross my mind until now and I kind of liked this idea.

The sun was set when we arrived, and the others had already eaten.

Skye was sitting all alone at the other side of the fire. I felt anger rise in me and heat started to make its way to my cheeks. I wanted to tell that bitch what I've been meaning to.

Will pulled on my hand. "Ignore her, stay with me."

I nodded to him. He grabbed my hips and brought me closer to him, his tongue making its way into my mouth. In just one kiss, he managed to calm the storm that was raging inside of me.

Damien came to see us. He saw the mark on my neck and smirked.

"Hey guys, glad to see you. I was beginning to wonder where you were."

He handed us food they had kept for us while we were gone.

My grandmother came running to me. "Oh Leila! My treasure! I was so worried about you!"

I laughed; my grandmother always worried about me.

"Grandma, you don't need to worry about me. I'm not a child anymore."

She scolded me, "don't you run away like that again. You might not be a child, but I'm still your chieftess."

I hugged her. "Okay, okay. I promise."

I grabbed the food Damien was handing us and went to sit by the fire with Will. Since it was already evening, everyone had decided to make camp for the night.
I saw my grandmother pacing nervously, but I had no idea why. I thought maybe she was still tense from what had happened earlier. I decided to brush it off.

Will and I kept our distance from Skye. I noticed she was staring at us a few times, but decided it was not worth my energy. I stayed in Will's arms, basking in his scent, listening to his heart while watching the stars sparkle. Right now, in his arms, I could really feel this is where I belonged.

When nightfall came, we went to his tent. I curled up in his arms. He wrapped his strong arms around me, laying soft kisses on my neck. If I had to describe what paradise felt like, this was it.

I woke up with Leila still in my arms. She was both strong and sexy. She was my mate, my Luna. I wanted to worship her every day like the queen she was to me. Her sweet scent of citrus and jasmine was intoxicating, and I couldn't get enough of her. Even now, still sleeping, she managed to bring me to my knees. I buried my nose in the crook of her neck, being careful not to wake her up.

Her lips curved up while her eyes were still closed as she whispered, "Hmmm… morning, Will."

I grinned, knowing she was enjoying this moment as much as I did. I removed the hair that was in my way and started kissing her neck. I took care to let my lips linger on her soft skin with each kiss. I slowly made my way to the back of her neck. When I removed the hair on the nape of her neck, I noticed a mark in the form of a diamond. I hadn't noticed it earlier since it was hidden under her hair. It looked like a golden diamond, almost glowing, compared to her lovely tawny skin. I traced the shape of it with my finger and she shivered.

"What's that?" I asked. It was the same as the diamond mark she had when she was in her wolf form. I had never seen anything like it.

Leila shrugged her shoulders. "I was born with it."

A birthmark… I wondered what it meant.

She asked shyly, "do you like it?"

I kissed her birthmark. "I love every part of you, my love."

A voice called from outside my tent.

"Hey lovers, are you up already? I wouldn't want to come inside and stumble onto something I'm not supposed to!"

Damien was laughing heartily, and I could hear Blake laughing by his side, too.

"We'll be there in a minute," I answered. I wouldn't want them to see Leila like this. I wish we didn't have to leave. But I knew we still had a dragon to find. That is… if the legends were true.

I got dressed and exited the tent. Leila came out a few minutes after.

Damien and Blake had already packed all their stuff. Ravynne was helping Leila pack our stuff as well. I kept an eye on Skye, who was keeping her distance. It was better that way. I was still angry at her for what she had done. I could have lost my mate because of her. I would never forgive her. I was still wary she might try stuff to get us away one from another.

At least, now that the mating process was done. I smiled to myself. That also meant Leila would fall into heat in a few days. I wondered if she had thought about that. I knew it was quick, but I was already looking forward to having pups with her. I knew she was the one I wanted to spend my life with. She turned her head my way, laying her deep chocolate brown eyes on me. Her stare held all the love she felt for me, and secrets deeper than the deepest sea. I only wished to drown myself in them.

"Hey Will! Coming?" Blake was calling.

I nodded and started walking towards the waterfall. Ravynne was walking with Blake and Damien. Leila was walking by my side, and Skye was walking alone in the back. She was still complaining, but nobody cared about her by this point. She had been complaining about all and nothing since the beginning of the trip, trying to have everyone's pity for herself. I just thought she wanted all the attention and was jealous of anyone getting more than her.

We arrived shortly to the edge of a big cave hidden behind the waterfall. It was very tall, and I couldn't see anything past the first few feet, as there was no light inside. Small crystals could be seen growing through the rocks. I held my breath as I felt this place impose respect onto us. An icy breath emanated from the cave. I wondered if this was really the lair of Ladon. I held on to Leila's hand as we started to walk inside the cave. Ravynne and Skye made sure to stay close to the group. They were the only ones who didn't have an improved night vision.

The cave soon opened into a wide chamber. The air was freezing, and steam escaped our mouths as we breathed. I gasped as I spotted this immense rock statue at the center of the room. Could it be the legends were true? At the center of the room was an immense dragon statue. He was curled up on itself, sleeping. He didn't have a hundred heads like in the legends, but he did have six heads. I approached cautiously. He looked so real! Every detail was spot on! I could even see each scale on his skin. He truly looked like he was sleeping and could open his eyes anytime. The statue was frozen cold to the touch. I had to remove my fingers as they were beginning to tingle from the cold.

"There he is…" whispered Ravynne in awe.

"It's only a statue," commented Leila.

Ravynne shook her head. "Don't be deceived by appearances."

She made her way to the other side of the dragon statue.

"Come Leila, my treasure. We must wake him up." she gestured to Leila. Then she looked at us. "It is important that Leila and I don't get interrupted. The wake-up ritual must be completed in silence for the dragon to awaken in peace."

"What will happen if the ritual gets interrupted?" I asked.

"I'm not sure," she answered. "But we might not live to tell the tale, so let's make this correctly."

We looked at one and another, nodding seriously.

Leila and her grandmother held hands together and started to recite an incantation. "Expergefactio, onis, Valentia…"

I stood still as I watched them reciting, eyes closed. Soon, a warm energy started to circle around them, and everywhere in the chamber. I was amazed at the power emanating from them both. It reminded me of when they cast the spell on my father. I was impressed then, and I still was impressed. I wondered what it felt like. I closed my eyes and tried to focus on the mate bond I had with Leila. Immediately, I could feel what she was feeling. It was like I had this surge of power within me. I felt this fire, and this calmness at the same time. Like a silent storm raging inside. It was strong yet soothing at the same time.

Rocks started to fall from the statue, revealing magnificent scales! They were black with blueish-turquoise reflections. Every time I moved, the colors seemed to change as well, each scale flickering with a unique fire. I had never seen something that pretty in my life. Suddenly, one of the heads moved, more rock making its way to the ground. The eyes of one of the beast's head opened to reveal green reptilian eyes.

The dragon seemed calm; he was studying us. I sucked in a breath. Leila and Ravynne were still chanting their spell. The beast was not fully awaked, and they needed to finish the spell for the process to complete.

From the corner of my eye, I spotted Skye with a vicious smile on her face. She was advancing towards Leila with a dagger in her hand. My wolf jumped in my chest, my heart beating fast. I jumped close to Skye and grabbed her arm, making her drop the knife.

"Let me go!" she screamed, trying to free herself and pick up the knife.

Leila and Ravynne opened their eyes. The spell they were chanting had been broken and the energy that was flowing stopped.

"What were you about to do?" I asked, angry at her. How dared she attack my mate? I saw her sly face. I knew she did it on purpose. Did she really had the intention of killing her friend? My chest tightened. I knew she had been friends with Leila for a long time, but right now, all I wanted to do was to tear her apart.

Skye didn't have time to answer. That a rumbling growl filled the chamber. It was a bone-chilling screech that could be heard by the undead. A shiver of dread got down my spine. Ladon was awake, the remaining rocks falling to the ground. Standing on his paws, he was at least ten feet tall. He spread his wings, creating a gust of wind in the process. His tail was swinging violently, and Damien had to jump to avoid being swept by it. Ladon looked furious. His heads were focused on Skye. She was the one who screamed and stopped the ritual. He seemed to want to unleash his fury on her.

My pulse was racing. I clenched my jaw, trying to figure out what to do. Leila was on one side with her grandmother. Skye was trying to move away from the beast, but he was following her every move. Even Damien and Blake looked scared. The dragon's growls were way too loud for us to try to elaborate a plan.

Blake and Damien looked at each other and jumped on the creature. Damien tried to scratch the dragon with his nails, but its skin was too thick. Blake got his dagger out and stuck the blade into the tail. The dragon shrieked in pain and tried to bite Blake. He couldn't get all the way back, so he started to swing his tail even more violently, trying to shake the dagger out. He hit the walls of the cave with his tail, making boulders of rocks fall to the ground. Skye tried to take this moment of distraction to her advantage, but she stumbled on a rock and fell to the ground. The dragon saw that she had fallen and dived two of his powerful jaws at her. He was too fast for any of us to react. In an instant, Skye's screams filled the room as the dragon tore limbs and flesh from her. Leila was in her grandmother's arm, trying not to look at her friend. Luckily, her screams stopped soon enough. The beast devoured her flesh in a matter of seconds. Only blood and a few shreds of clothes stayed on the ground.

The beast was still furious and was now turning his attention to us.

"Remove your blade! It's only making it angrier," I shouted to Blake.

I was glad that my voiced reached Blake. The moment he removed the blade from the dragon's tail, he seemed to calm, at least a little.

I thought to myself. "If everything went well, Ladon would have awakened calm."

I looked up at Leila and an idea crossed my mind.

I concentrated to her through our mate bond. "Do you think you can soothe him?"

She looked at me with wide eyes. "soothe him"?

"Yes, he was supposed to be calm when he woke up, but the ritual got disrupted."

She nodded to me. "Okay I'll try something."

I loved her witching powers; she never ceased to amaze me.

Leila said something in her grandmother's ear. Seeing that Leila and Ravynne were going to cast a spell again, Damien used his vampire hypnotic powers on the dragon. Despite him being the vampire Lord, and overly powerful, the beast was resisting the pull. You could see him fight and try to break free. Damien gestured to Blake. He immediately joined him. With both using their full powers on him, the dragon had no choice but to give in. Ladon turned himself to face Damien and Blake. It looked as if he was studying them, and I was wondering what he could be thinking about.

Leila and Ravynne started chanting, but I couldn't hear what they were saying. I could, however, feel the warm breeze of their spell around us. Ladon immediately calmed itself.

"You need to go to him," Leila spoke in my head.

"Why?" I answered.

"He needs a master."

The words took me by surprise. I mean, I was an Alpha. But the master of an almighty dragon? This seemed unreal.

I walked towards Ladon. The beast was so majestic; I held my breath in front of such power. The beast turned one of its heads in my direction, and I wondered, for a moment, if it broke free from the spells. But sure enough, he was only observing me.

I approached the head that was the closest to me and brought my hand near his nose like you would do with a dog. He seemed to be taking in my scent.

I could feel my wolf trying to assert his Alpha position. I mean over a dragon?? It was craziness. I didn't know what spell Leila and her grandmother were casting, but it sure looked like it was powerful.

After a while, I felt my wolf holding his head high. I understood that the dragon had accepted my wolf and me as his master, however crazy that seemed. I was astounded when the beast rubbed his head in my hand and made a soft rumble. It looked like a baby cuddling with his mother. The only thing I could manage to do was to rub his neck with my other hand.

Ladon truly seemed pleased by the fact I was his new master. I was so shocked that I didn't even notice that Leila and Ravynne had stopped their spell casting. Damien and Blake were standing together, smiling. I guess that there was no need for magic powers anymore. The dragon was on our team now.

Chapter 15 (Will)

Island of Delos

I was so amazed by what happened with Ladon that I had completely forgotten what happened to Skye until I heard Damien talk to Leila.

"I'm so sorry for what happened to your friend."

I turned to face them, worried that Leila might need my support. I mean, I haven't known Skye for a long time, but Leila had known her for her entire life.

Leila's eyes were sad, but she wasn't crying.

"I… it's okay… I guess," she whispered.

I held her in my arms. "It's not okay, she was your friend. You have the right to be sad." I told her gently.

She raised her head to look at me, studying me with her lovely eyes.

"Even if she tried to set us apart?"

These words hurt but I nodded to her. "The past few days were not great. But she had been your friend for so many years."

She nodded, but then Blake added, "she did try to kill her, though."

Leila gasped. In the midst of the spell casting, she had not realized that Skye tried to stab her with a dagger.

I held her tight, and she relaxed in my arms. "Did she really?" she whispered.

"Yes…" I answered, "that's why the spell casting was broken. I stopped her, and she yelled."

Tears rolled down her cheeks. I could feel how devastated she was from our mate bond.

"I… can't believe…" she managed to say between the tears. But she didn't need to say more. We all knew what she meant. It was the trust of many years, a true friendship, crumbling apart in her heart. The feeling of betrayal, stronger than a typhoon, ravaging everything in its way. All I could do was to hold her in my arms so she didn't fall apart.

Ravynne was also shedding a few tears, but Blake, Damien, and me… well, we didn't know Skye for a long time. And I was still angry at the fact she tried to attack my mate with a dagger. Who knows what she would have done if I hadn't stopped her?

We waited for Leila to feel better. I made sure to wipe her tears away.

When she was fine, Damien broke the silence, "well, we've got one dragon now. There are still five of us."

"Think there's more dragons around?" Leila asked.

We all looked at each other, not really knowing what to do.

Ravynne pointed to Ladon. "Why don't you ask him?"

From the way they were all staring at me, it was clear they wanted me to ask the dragon.

"I don't… really know how to speak to a dragon."

I mean… Did I have to roar or something? I laughed at myself, thinking how ridiculous that would look.

Ravynne nodded. "You are its master now. If you concentrate on it, you should be able to talk to him."

I was taken aback from her comment. It was worth a try. I guess it could be a little bit like when I speak to Leila through our mate bond. Or like when I communicate with my wolf, just knowing what it feels and wants, even though I don't speak wolf. I nodded to her and then turned to Ladon.

He was sitting, looking my way, as if waiting for an order from me.

I approached one of his heads and rested my forehead against it. He was cold to the touch, but not as much as when he was a statue. I closed my eyes and concentrated on him.

I could feel a cold wind rising inside of me. It was as if I could feel Ladon inside of me. I wasn't sure how to speak to him, but I had a feeling that my wolf did. Considering he became the Alpha a little earlier.

I tried to concentrate on what I wanted to know: were there other dragons nearby so that we could ride to the Island of Delos?

I had this strangest feeling, like my wolf was conversing with Ladon. It was the strangest thing ever. I was used to conversing with my wolf, or with my mate, but not to witness a conversation between my wolf and another person. I was just a spectator inside of my head.

A moment after, Ladon started to move his head away from mine. I opened my eyes and saw him get back a few steps. He stood on his back legs and screeched in a high-pitched tone. He moved away from the spot where he had been sleeping to reveal a big opening in the floor. It looked like the cave was continuing further down the floor. It was a very big opening with a slight slope. We ventured down, followed by Ladon.

We soon arrived at a gigantic chamber. My mouth was wide open. I simply couldn't move. In front of us were dozens of dragons. Some were flying and others were resting. There were babies feeding from their mothers. It looked like they were drinking a milk-like substance from their mother's mouth, a little like some birds do. I was fascinated by them. Their colors varied a lot, going from black to white. Some of them being brown, even golden, and others being gray. Part of them had multiple colors, and others had only one. A few dragons even had multiple tails, or two heads. But Ladon was the only one with six heads. I wondered if he was the last of his species. It must be very hard to be the only one of your kind. I knew I would be lonely. I wondered if dragons could mix. Like lions and tigers sometimes do.

It was simply beautiful, as if we stumbled into a completely different world; one we didn't even suspect existed.

"Wow," whispered Leila.

"How are we going to choose the ones we need?" asked Blake.

"We are not the ones choosing," said Ravynne. "*They* will be choosing us."

I wondered what she meant by that.

I didn't have to wonder for a long time. Ladon started to growl loudly. He seemed to be communicating with the other dragons. I wondered what he was telling them. He looked like he was somehow in charge. Was there a hierarchy amongst dragons? Did they have an Alpha like we had in our packs? I realized there was so little I knew about them. I mean, well… just earlier I thought they existed only in legends, so of course, I didn't know a lot about them! With the size of the beasts, you would think everyone would have seen them!

A few seconds later, multiple dragons landed all around us. They came close, observing us, taking in our scent. Now, I understood what Ravynne meant. They were choosing us, deciding if they should come with us or not on our journey. Some of them went away, I guess they weren't interested in joining. But soon enough, some stayed, each one seemingly choosing their teammate.

Damien had a majestic white dragon by his side. He was standing tall and proud and seemed both kind and strong. Ravynne looked like she was getting to know her dragon. It was gray and white, with two tails. Its skin looked old and cracked, but he looked very gentle and curious. Blake had a young black dragon that seemed eager to jump right into the adventure. He wasn't tall, but he had an energy in his eyes that showed how committed he was. As for Leila, she had a beautiful brown and golden dragon by her side. She looked strong, and her scales shone like jewels.

Ladon stepped towards Leila's dragon and rubbed his heads against her. I guess it was a female dragon, then, I smiled to myself. What a fitting match, that my lover's dragon would also be my dragon's lover. They looked at each other with such intensity, they must have been staring at each other's soul. Nobody could come between them. In this moment, I felt a sudden need to hold my Leila in my arms. To look at her and cherish her as much as Ladon was loving his lover.

"Her name is Cara," Leila pushed through my head.

"How do you know?" I answered.

"I just do," she replied.

I guess it was the same with how I communicate with Ladon.

Unable to hold myself anymore, I closed the distance between me and my sweet Leila. I grabbed her by the waist. She leaned into my embrace effortlessly. Her soft lips parted as I kissed her. No words were necessary, I could feel her heart beat strong in her chest all the way through mine. I knew she felt it too. This was my paradise, my salvation. I was drunk from her love and never wanted to let go.

Leila's POV

My cheeks felt hot when we broke the kiss. A part of me knew everybody was watching us. A part of me didn't care. My body was burning with desire for this man. I only wished to drown myself in his blue eyes and sink myself into his arms. How I wish I could stop time just for a moment.

Soon enough, I noticed that everybody was mounting on their dragon's backs. Cara and Ladon broke their embrace. Will gently helped me get on Cara's back, before mounting his own dragon.

Cara started to fly, and I could feel pulled with each wing flap. We exited the cave in no time at all. Soon, I started to see the forest beneath us, getting smaller. I was dizzy from height and my heart was beating fast. I held on tight to Cara.

I felt a wind of comfort coming from inside, Will was sending it through our bond and I immediately calmed.

"Don't worry," he said through my head. "You'll get used to it."

I wondered how he was so sure about this. As if reading my mind, he added, "I used to do the same, the first time I flew with the vampires. I'm used to it now."

I only hoped he was right.

We flew up northeast, passing over the Melian nymph's sacred grove. Even from the top, I could clearly make out the Tree of Life still blooming, contrasting with the dark leafless trees around it. November had slowly crept in. On the ground could still be seen some dead leaves but they were graying out. Everything felt dark and lifeless in the forest below. I guess that was why I've always been told it was the month of the dead.

We continued flying a little more. I was now enjoying the ride, feeling the wind in my hair. Ladon and Cara kept flying together, crossing paths. They seemed to be having an aerial dance together. You could feel how much they loved one another. It made me wish I was in Will's arms right now, longing for his warmth and kisses.

The dragons were flying fast, and soon enough, we saw a big floating island up ahead. We could also see a powerful storm raging all around it. Dark clouds circled it. Strong winds were making rocks and other debris fly, and you could spot occasional lightning striking. I looked down below and saw this deep crevice. Inside it was this very huge dragon, bigger than anything I had ever seen! I guess it must be the legendary Kholkikos. The dragon had two huge black horns on each side of its head. His eyes were all black, and the sight of it made the hair on the back of my neck raise. His mouth was slightly open, to let his breath flow to the island over him, allowing me to glimpse at his sharp teeth. He was all white, and to my surprise, he didn't have scales, but was covered by feathers. He was lying down, his long tail curled up around him. His two gigantic wings were deployed, as if making him a blanket. He was truly magnificent, and at least ten times bigger than our dragons, if not more. He was the protector of this island. If his breath only was strong enough to make this island float, and create that storm, then I would never want to try to confront him.

We all stopped, assessing the island and its storm. I knew we had no choice but to get through, but I still couldn't help having second thoughts about this. The storm was stronger than I could ever imagine. Going right through would probably be difficult, even for dragons. The winds were too powerful, and we would probably get blown to the side. Flying against the winds and slowly making our way in, was probably a better idea. Although it would take us more time, it was probably the only way we could manage to do it.

I couldn't help but to wonder what kinds of treasures must be hidden on this island for it to be protected by such a powerful dragon.

We started to fly into the storm. I was almost swept away from Cara by a strong gust of wind but managed to hold myself in place. I could feel Cara struggling, putting all her energy into fighting the storm. Around me, I saw debris flying around. I was only hoping that we wouldn't get hit by anything. My heart was beating fast, and I was grabbing so hard on Cara that my arms hurt. I glimpsed around and saw the other dragons were also struggling, but slowly making their way through the storm. The lightning was dancing with us, and striking way too close for comfort. Thunder was rumbling so loudly; I could feel it reverberate through my body. Time seemed to stay still as we made our way through the storm. I couldn't wait to be on the other side.

Soon, I felt like I could begin to see the end of the storm. Suddenly, Cara plunged downwards, headfirst. The sudden movement got me off her back, and I was now falling fast.

"Will," I screamed.

I closed my eyes, as the only thing I could think of was that I was going to die. I didn't know why Cara did that; we were so close to the island. I wondered if I would be hit by some rocks first or fall to the ground below before. Either way, I knew it would be painful. Luckily, I knew that it would be quick.

I braced myself as I felt something coming my way. But instead of hurting, I recognized Will's scent.

"Got you!" was all I heard in my ear. Those were the sweetest words I had ever heard. I grabbed on to one of Ladon's head, Will's arms around me, also holding on to the dragon. Ladon was still flying down fast, and I realized he was going after Cara. I looked down, and noticed that Cara wasn't flying downwards, she was falling, unconscious.

Ladon was trying hard to reach her. I wondered for a moment if he was strong enough to have both of us on his back, and to grab another dragon. I knew for sure that Ladon would do whatever it took to save the one he loved, even if it meant he gave his life. I only wished it didn't come to that, but I could understand, as I would do the same for Will.

He finally got close enough to grab Cara with his paws. The sudden increase in weight seemed to be hard on him. I knew he was strong at the instant I first saw him, but he was even stronger than I thought. He began flapping his wings with such force that he managed to get all of us back up, to the island, on the other side of the storm.

We landed on the island, and I was glad to get down and have my two feet on the ground again. As soon as I got off from Ladon, two strong arms encircled me. My heart was beating strong as Will laid kisses on my neck.

"I was so scared of losing you again," he whispered in my ear. "You're beginning to make a habit out of it," he gently scolded.

I turned to face him, losing myself in his eyes.

"Sorry," I answered.

He smiled and kissed me passionately. He roamed my back with his hands. In this moment, I felt like nothing else mattered. I was surrounded by love and couldn't care about anything else.

But a cry of pain got me back to reality. Cara was still lying unconscious on the ground, and Ladon was desperate for her to wake up. All his sadness and ache could be felt through his cries. I got close to Cara, feeling her vital signs. I could feel a faint pulse. She was so weak.

"She needs to heal," I muttered.

I didn't have to say anything more. My grandmother nodded and came closer.

"Then you know what needs to be done."

I got up and grabbed her hands.

Together, we started chanting our spell. This was one of the spells I loved casting. As we chanted the words, I felt the usual warm wind wrap around me; the energy flowing all around and inside of me. There was no given rule as to how long we needed to cast the spell. We just knew when to stop. My grandmother called it the witch instinct. It was as if we could communicate with magic itself, channeling the energy, and getting feedback from it as to when it was enough.

I always lost track of time when casting a spell. As if my mind was so busy with the magic that nothing else was important. When we stopped chanting, I opened my eyes.

Everyone was staring, all watching Cara, waiting for her to move. I touched her belly and noticed her heartbeat was stronger. She was getting better, that was for sure.

She emitted a soft growl and slowly opened her eyes. Immediately, Ladon got close to her and rubbed his heads against her with love. I could feel how relieved he was, and I had to say, I was thankful as well that she was better.

Chapter 16 (Eurynomos)

The sacred sword

Her eyes drowned in defeat. The fighting force that inhabited them yesterday was almost dead now. They were almost void of life. Being chained up, tortured, without being fed, showed even better results than I had hoped. I rejoiced at this sight. I couldn't wait to have my way with her. This would be delightful for sure. I could almost taste her on my lips.

Her wrists were still bleeding. She was staring at the floor. Her hair was in disarray and filthy with dirt and blood. Feathers from her wings lingered on the floor, where she had lost them during torture. This was surely the most beautiful sight I've ever had. I didn't want to admit the sight of her was making the fire rise in my blood.

She wasn't given anything to drink. I knew the moment when she couldn't resist drinking my blood was coming. After that, I will have all that I crave. She will beg for me to take her. She will do my bidding, and she'll be thanking me for it.

Slowly, she raised her eyes and seemed to realize I was in her cell. I couldn't resist but to get close to her. I licked the blood that was bleeding from her wrists. It tasted so good. She didn't even flinch, only watched me. Not that she could move as her hands were chained to the wall, and she was hanging from the chains.

"Hey there sugar... are you thirsty?" I asked with a wicked smile. "I swear you'll beg for more."
She didn't answer anything. Her parched lips cracked and dirty. My body was over hers against the wall, but she didn't fight. I slowly licked her dried lips. I wanted more.
She was so numb from the torture; she didn't even react. I was aroused by her more than I wanted to admit to myself. I already felt my cock hard, ready for her.

I took a step back, trying to sound as nice as I could.

"Well, little girl, why don't I give you what you crave?"

I took the cup of blood that was on the table nearby and got it to her lips. She was so desperate; she was so thirsty and dying. I watched her gulp down every droplet of blood, not leaving a single one.

I watched her crisp in pain, as the blood affected her body and slowly began to change her. Her eyes were now a dark black color, and I could smell how aroused she was becoming.

"Good girl," I whispered as I undid her ties so she could be free.

I took a break from reading and got back to the balcony. I watched as the fighters kept killing wave after wave of enemies. The bodies were piling up on the floor in front of the castle. Puddles of blood were forming, and a metallic scent was rising to the balcony. I could only imagine how it smelled down at ground level.

I had the impression the waves of orcs and goblins were getting bigger. I wondered if our fighters were going to be fine. A few of them were injured, but we hadn't lost a lot so far. Luckily, Steven was fine. Sure, I didn't want anything to happen to the others either, but he was my main concern.

Kate came outside and joined me.

"Well, would you look at that." She pointed to the fighters.

I followed her finger and recognized his sexy ass from earlier.

"It seems he's done with the girls and decided to join the fight." I laughed.

Kate giggled. "It seems that Jake is able to take orders from his queen."

"Think they'll be fine?"

I had to ask; I couldn't help myself. I was getting anxious. It seemed Eurynomos's army only got stronger, and I worried we might be overrun.

Kate sighed, "I hope so."

She pulled me inside the castle. "Come, it's no use watching them. You're better off trying to find something in those books."

"You're right," I answered.

I knew she was right. I loved to read books. But I had read so many of them now, searching for solutions to break the curse or to stop Eurynomos. Yet, I knew the correct thing to do was to keep reading until I found something.

It was already dark. My eyes were sore from reading. I wanted to close that book when I stumbled onto something interesting. It was a part talking about Ravynne's pack again. It seemed that it's a very ancient sacred pack, very close to the moon goddess. The moon goddess herself gave the witches their powers. That's how the humans came to be able to use magic in the first place.

Now, as I found out earlier, they were responsible for keeping Eurynomos sealed, and they failed at it. But this book explained that in order to retain Eurynomos in the underworld, they had to sacrifice a young man from their clan. His blood had to be given in order to keep the demon away. It was a tradition upheld generation after generation. But at one point, the young man's parents couldn't get themselves to kill their son. Together, the pack had a meeting, and they decided to give up their role as keepers of the demon and flee. That's how they became a rogue pack in the very beginning.

They say that for every generation, a member of the clan was born under a blessed night.

That person was then the most precious member of the pack. They had to be cherished until the day comes that he or she is to be sacrificed.

Now that seemed like such a cruel fate. I couldn't even imagine what it must feel like. I wondered who was born on a blessed night in Ravynne's pack for the current generation. Could this have a link to the riddle?

"… a beloved treasure will have to be sacrificed."

This couldn't be a coincidence! I needed to say that to Kate right away so that she could say it to Damien.

The dragons had been resting. Cara seemed to feel better now. Ladon has been by her side ever since we've been back on the land. As for myself, I was enjoying some time with my sweet Leila. I loved her so much, I couldn't bear to be apart from her. I was already planning on taking her back to the pack once all of this was over. I was already yearning to build a family with her. Having our own pups, living happily together, leading the pack and protecting one another. I wondered if our children would be born with her witch's powers. So many things I wanted to know about her, but for now, I closed my eyes as I burrowed my nose in the crook of her neck.

"Ravynne, can I talk to you?" I heard Damien speak.

I opened my eyes and noticed he had a strange look on his face. Ravynne followed him a little further. I watched as they spoke. Ravynne looked like she was agitated, and I wondered what they were talking about.

When they were done talking, I rose and went to talk with Damien.

"Hey, what was that about?" I asked him.

He stared at the ground, then back at me.

"Nothing of importance."

I knew he was lying. He had been dating my sister long enough for me to know.

"Come on, I know you better than that. Spit it out."

He shook his head. "I'm sorry, I can't."

He turned around and tried to go, but I grabbed his arm.

"I know you're hiding something important. Why won't you tell me?" I snarled at him.

He was a vampire Lord. It was no use of me to try to use my Alpha powers on him. It wouldn't work. He looked at me with intensity in the eyes.

"You will know in time."

He got his arm free and walked further.

I didn't like it. I knew something was off. But I trusted Damien. I knew that if he said I would know later, then it was true.

Blake came by, running. "The orcs are on the island."

I ran to him.

"What? How is it possible? It was so hard to get here in the first place!"

"It seems a portal has been opened on the island," answered Blake.

I cursed.

"Okay, no time to waste, then. We need to find the sacred grove of Ares. Any idea where that might be?" I asked.

Ravynne pointed to some tall trees a little to the East.

"We should go there. I feel magic coming from there," she answered.

It was the best lead that we had.

We started to walk towards the forest. The dragons were free to go wherever they wanted, but they seemed to have decided to stick around. I wasn't about to complain. Dragons were powerful creatures, so having them on our side was a great advantage. Plus, when we'll want to get off this island, we'll need their help. The sound of the orcs in the distance kept us on our edges. I wasn't sure exactly where they were, but I knew they weren't that far. I only hoped we wouldn't have to fight them.

As we walked to the East, the forest began to be thicker. I could feel the air charged with energy, even if I didn't have any magic in me. My wolf was getting restless. There was no denying this was the right place. We walked for a while and arrived at a strange wooden door carved into a cave. It was the strangest of things, as there were no buildings on the island, and so I wondered who would put a door on a cave. And what's more, a door this huge. Nevertheless, I knew this was the place we were looking for.

We entered and discovered this place was an ancient temple. From the symbols decorating the walls, it seemed to be a place where vampires and werewolves got together. Which seemed very strange, as vampires and werewolves had been enemies for so many centuries before. This temple surely was very old then, dating from before the first war. I wondered what secrets held this place.

Rooms were carved into the rocks. It crumbled with dust. Torches hung around the walls.

Ravynne and Leila took care of lighting them, providing us with some light. Not that I needed it, but it was easier this way. There wasn't a lot of rooms. We knew we were in the right place when we stumbled upon this big room with an altar at the center. A big hole at the center of the roof allowed for the moonlight to enter and shine on the altar.

At one side, we saw a sword floating in the air.

"Think it's the sacred sword?" I asked.

Leila nodded. "Surely."

Getting closer, it looked even more powerful than from afar. The blade was encrusted with symbols I had never seen. It looked like it was made from one of the finest metals. It looked both sharp and strong. The handle was made of gold, encrusted with amethysts. I wondered how it managed to float in the air. I tried to grab it, but I couldn't get my hands near it.

"It's protected by a spell," Ravynne spoke.

Huh… I didn't know a lot about spells.

"Think you can remove it?" I asked Leila.

She shrugged her shoulders. "I could try."

But Ravynne shook her head.

"That spell is quite powerful, it can't be removed just by anyone."

Well, that wasn't good. If Leila and her grandmother couldn't remove the spell, I wondered how we would manage to get the sword. We all stood there, searching for a solution.

Damien spoke, "remember what Bianca said?"

I looked at him with questioning eyes. Bianca said a lot of things frankly. I loved my sister, but I couldn't remember everything she said.

He continued, "she said vampires and werewolves had to unite themselves in order to break the curse."

Right, she did say that.

"Do you think maybe we need to unite in order to get the sword?" I asked.

Damien answered, "Well, it's worth a shot."

He got closer to the sword and then shouted, "hey! I know those symbols! This is ancient vampiric language."

He then continued, "it says a mighty wolf needs to enter the circle as the formula is recited by a creature of the night… I guess that's me."

I laughed.

"Funny that even your ancestors described themselves as creatures of the night."

Damien punched me on the shoulder.

"So, does that mean I need to shift into my wolf?" I asked.

Damien shrugged his shoulders.

"I guess you should try."

I got in a dark corner of the room to remove my clothes. I didn't mind getting naked in front of Leila. But I didn't want to get naked in front of everyone. I quickly let myself change into my wolf form. My wolf had been restless since we got near this place. It felt good to let him loose.

I was amazed at how different this place looked now that I was in my wolf form. Symbols appeared to be visible only with my wolf vision and not with my human eyes.

"You should see that," I pushed through Leila's mind.

She giggled. "Come here my big bad wolf, let me run my fingers through that soft fur of yours."

I could feel how much she longed for me through our mate bond.

I made my way back to them. Leila got down and started to pet my wolf. It felt so good to have her fingers in my fur. I closed my eyes as I rubbed my muzzle against her. I could feel her wolf longing for me. I couldn't wait for all of this to be done with and to be able to spend time alone with her.

"Hey lovers, can we get on with it?" an amused Damien asked.

I smirked at him, or however wolves could smirk, anyway.

The sword seemed to glow with a strange power. I could clearly see where I was supposed to grab it. I guess it was only visible to wolves.

I nodded to Damien, and he started reciting the words.

"*Puterile care protejează această sabie sacră, pleacă.*"

I had no idea what those words meant, but I could see the energy protecting the sword flickering. It was faltering just enough for me to have time to grab the sword in my mouth.

The sword was heavier than I thought, and the blade gave a loud thud as it hit the floor.

"Careful there, wolf boy." Damien winked at me.

He grabbed the sword from me. I changed back to my human form and got dressed before joining with them again.

They were all studying the sword when I arrived.

"Good job," Leila said with a smile.

Everybody seemed to be happy, but Ravynne still had a worried look on her face.

"What do we need to do with it?" Blake asked.

"Hmm… let's think back to the riddle," Leila answered.

I thought back to the riddle.

"To undo a sin, committed centuries ago. A floating island, in the middle of a thundering storm. A sacred sword must be found," I recited.

"Well, we already did all of that," Blake spoke happily.

I nodded to him. "I guess it leaves the last part. A beloved treasure will have to be sacrificed…"

Although I didn't understand what it meant, I had a feeling it was related to the center of the room.

"I guess it's related to the altar over there." I pointed to them.

They nodded excitingly.

I noticed that Ravynne was further away, with Damien. She didn't look happy at all, and Damien was speaking with her. I wanted to go see them, but we started to hear loud bangs on the wooden door.

Leila's eyes widened. "The orcs! They must be trying to get in!"

"We must be quick, then!" Blake answered.

We rushed to the altar, studying it. The bangs began to get louder and louder, crumbs of rocks falling from the roof onto the ground around us. My heart was beating fast. I was desperately trying to figure out what to do, before the orcs would be able to get through the door.

Leila shouted, "I see symbols!"

I had no idea what she saw. I only guessed she could see them because of her witch's powers.

Damien and Ravynne came closer to the altar with us as the bangs continued to echo around us.

Chapter 17 (Leila)

The sacrifice

I lowered myself to study the symbols further.

"To right what was wrong, the one born under a blessed night, treasured by all, the jewel of them all, must be sacrifice. Only when it's done, will the sin be forgiven."

Those words resonated inside of me. Somehow, I felt like I've known them before. I had the feeling down there that I could solve them. The words kept playing in my head.

Rocks kept crumbling around us, the orcs trying to make their way inside. This was our chance to break the curse and maybe prevent Eurynomos from entering this world. We couldn't afford not to succeed.

I stood back up.

"What does it say?" asked Will eagerly. Blake was also waiting eagerly. Yet somehow, my grandmother was looking away, and Damien was with her.

That's when it hit me. My heart stopped at the realization of what this meant. I took a step back, my mouth falling open. I couldn't believe it, yet I couldn't escape the truth. Tears started to roll silently on my cheeks.

I looked at my grandmother, whispering, "you knew."

She turned to face me, a guilty look on her face, tears falling down her cheeks. She didn't say anything, only nodded.

"What?" asked Will, already running to me.

My hands were shaking, as I removed the hair hiding my birthmark showing my neck to everyone.

"A beloved treasure must be sacrificed," I whispered.

My grandmother's voice was trembling, "I didn't want it to be true. I hoped we discovered something else."

Will screamed at the top of his lungs, "no! This can't be!"

Damien spoke softly, "that's what Bianca thought… Their pack is ancient Will. They're linked to the goddess, and to the demon… I'm sorry, Will."

Will swung his arm violently through the air. "There has to be another way!"

I could feel the desperation through our mate bond. I didn't want to die.

My grandmother spoke weakly, "I always knew, with her diamond shape birthmark. One person was always born with it, one generation after the other… That's why we became a rogue pack in the first place." Her voice broke towards the end of her sentence.

I was so shocked, I couldn't move. Will was desperate to find another way.

"Then let's leave now! We'll stay a rogue pack!" Will shouted. "As long as I'm with you, I'll be fine."

Blake answered in disbelief, "what about your old pack? What about your sister, Bianca?"

Damien added, "what about the castle, and your sister Kate, and our baby growing inside of her?"

There was sadness inside of Will's eyes. I knew he didn't want to do this.

"Are we to let a demon take control of the world?" I asked Will softly.

Will grabbed my hand tenderly and squeezed it. All around us, rocks were falling to the ground.

"I'm sorry, Will, this has to be done!" screamed Blake. He tried to grab the sacred sword, but Will ripped it out of his hands.

"Don't you dare approach her," he snarled at them. His wolf was growling violently. He put his arms on both sides to protect me.

How I wished things could be different. Time was pressing. We didn't have another solution. I couldn't believe how cruel fate was.

I heard Damien speak to Will, "I know how it feels. The army is already assaulting the castle… There's been reports of the demon's army everywhere… I'm so sorry, Will."

I approached Will softly. He turned to face me. I wrapped my arms around his shoulders. I knew what needed to be done. There was no way we could let the demon win. It was my pack's ancestors' duties for centuries; it was my duty. My fate had been sealed since I was born. There was no use trying to run away from it. I wouldn't let the world crumble under the power of a demon.

Tears were rolling down on Will's cheeks. I grabbed his face with my hands, bringing his mouth to mine. We kissed softly, tears tasting salty in my mouth. I was trembling from all my body. In front of me crumbled my dream of a family, of a future, of everything I ever wanted.

I grabbed Will's hand holding the sword and brought the point to my chest. Will was crying, shaking his head.

"Leila... please, don't," his voice strangled, "we can find another way."

"Please Will, it must be done. At least, let it be by you..."

I held my hand firmly on the handle of the sword, on top of his.

"I want the last thing I see to be your eyes. Know that I will always be yours."

He was crying hard now, shaking his head in denial of what needed to be done.

I kissed him one last time. As we kissed, I leaned forward towards him; the blade piercing my skin, sending a sharp pain through my body. I didn't break the kiss. I wanted him to know how much I loved him, even while the blade tore my flesh apart. I could feel warm blood flowing down on my legs. I soon felt I couldn't hold my own weight anymore, but Will grabbed me in his arms. He continued to push on the sword against his will, crying in sobs.

My body felt cold, but Will's body kept me warm.

My head felt light, and my eyes started to close, even though I never wanted to stop looking at the man I loved.

"I will always love you with all that I am," I whispered.

I smiled as I felt myself drift away, knowing he felt the same as I did.

I couldn't believe she managed to smile in a moment like this. She wasn't breathing anymore. I held on to the woman I loved more than anything in the world. I didn't want to let go of her. The pain was so intense, never in my life had I imagined it'd be possible to hurt so much. To lose someone so dear to me. She was my everything. My wolf was hurting, the mate bond was breaking. I screamed with all that I could, a howl of desperation. Nothing could express the pain I was feeling.

I stayed there, watching her closed eyes, knowing they would never open again.

I kept whispering to her, "I will only love you."

Hoping that with some kind of magic, she could still hear me. Who knew, maybe she could even wake up? Maybe this was all a nightmare, and I will wake up?

Cara growled in pain, followed by Ladon and the other dragons. I knew everybody was watching me, but I didn't care. Nothing mattered. All that mattered was Leila. My sweet love, my everything. Without her, I was lost. I couldn't live anymore.

The sound of wood breaking resonated through the room. The orcs had finally succeeded in breaking the door. Damien and Blake were helping Ravynne onto her dragon.

"Will, come on, we need to go!" Blake shouted.

But I didn't care. I didn't want to leave her.

"You're the only one for me," I whispered to her, hugging tightly her body that was already getting cold.

I was sitting at the castle with Kate when I felt it. It was as if something was broken. All of a sudden, I found I wasn't linked to Eurynomos anymore. I also felt a surge of power inside of me, as if something missing had been returned after years of being taken away. I never felt this great. That meant that Will and the others had succeeded. I was so happy; this was a great victory for us! At least now we had a fighting chance against the demon.

The only thing I saw before the link with Eurynomos was broken, was a map hung on a wall. On it, I could see Montréal, and a big cross on it, telling me the location of the only entrance to the Underworld. It seemed the way to get to the Underworld was at a subway station in downtown Montréal.

I turned to Kate and told her immediately, so she could tell Damien. We needed them to come to the castle so we could regroup and plan our next moves.

I got a phone call almost immediately from my mother. She was screaming with joy. My father had miraculously gotten better. He had woken up, was slowly beginning to drink and eat again. With some luck, he would be out of bed in a few days.

This was great news; everything was starting to look better again.

Arius rushed inside the throne room, followed by Elashor. A few warriors were with them, including my sweet Steven.
"Quick! The enemies are flowing! We won't be able to hold them down."

I watched as Amaliel licked her fingers. She was so graciously naughty. Never would I have hoped for such a delicious little angel. She was executing everything I asked her with such grace. All her body was so sinful, I could never get enough of watching her cum. I thrust into her, again and again, as I never wanted to stop. I was getting addicted to her, but I would never admit it.

Hours passed, and I decided to let her rest. She was beautiful, my own little angel of death.
Suddenly, I felt something wrong. I got up from my bed, leaving Amaliel, already begging for me to return. I had more urgent matters to attend to. I went to look at the magical sphere that was floating near the portal. Sure enough, it was gone. The bitch had managed to free herself. It didn't matter, though. My invasion was well underway. The main portal was almost completely opened. It was only a matter of time before I could get into the world of the living and reign over everything. Now, with an angel by my side as well, I would be unstoppable. I laughed as I made my way back to please my little angel. I was already relishing in anticipation.

The orcs were rushing in, screaming, like the grotesque beasts they were. I couldn't care less. I didn't want to let go of my love.

Damien screamed at me, "come, we need to go! Quick! We need to regroup with Bianca for our next steps."

Had they already forgotten the sacrifice she made for them? Was I to leave her here, unburied? What would those orcs do to her body? Rage was growing in my heart. They were not worth it! Nobody was worth it! She shouldn't have done it. Why did she do it?

"Why?" I screamed from the bottom of my soul. I would never have an answer. All that was left was pain, sadness and anger.

Damien called, "we know the entrance to the Underworld is in Montréal. In a subway station. Come!"

Bigger rocks started to fall from the roof. Dragons used their bodies to try to protect me from getting crushed. But even the pain from getting crushed by a falling boulder wouldn't be as bad as the pain from losing my mate. I had never felt such despair. All sounds around me were cut off, as if I was underwater.

The orcs stormed in the room and started attacking the dragons. Damien was on his dragon, shouting to me. I could see his mouth opened, talking to me, but couldn't hear what he was saying.

Ladon was looking at me, pleading with me to come. I kissed Leila's cold cheek one last time. I swear to you, Leila. I will avenge you. I will not let your death be in vain. Eurynomos will pay for your death.

A word from the author

Hi!

I hope you enjoyed my book. I'm always happy to hear what you have to say about it, so don't forget to leave a review.

Check out my website and subscribe to my mailing list at daniellephauthor.com

All will unravel itself in The Fallen, the last book of this trilogy. You can grab your copy today, on Amazon.

Victory comes at a cost. Heroes rise and fall, and sometimes, death is a salvation.

Will they escape the cruel hands of fate?

https://www.amazon.com/dp/B0B7QJHKTP

Want to know more about the origins of Leila's pack? Delve into an ancient world full of love, lust, deception, and death. Discover the truth about the people who were called the Goddess's Wards.

https://www.amazon.com/dp/B0BPRGP9L7

Please leave a review on amazon and Goodreads!

Thanks for your support

Danielle

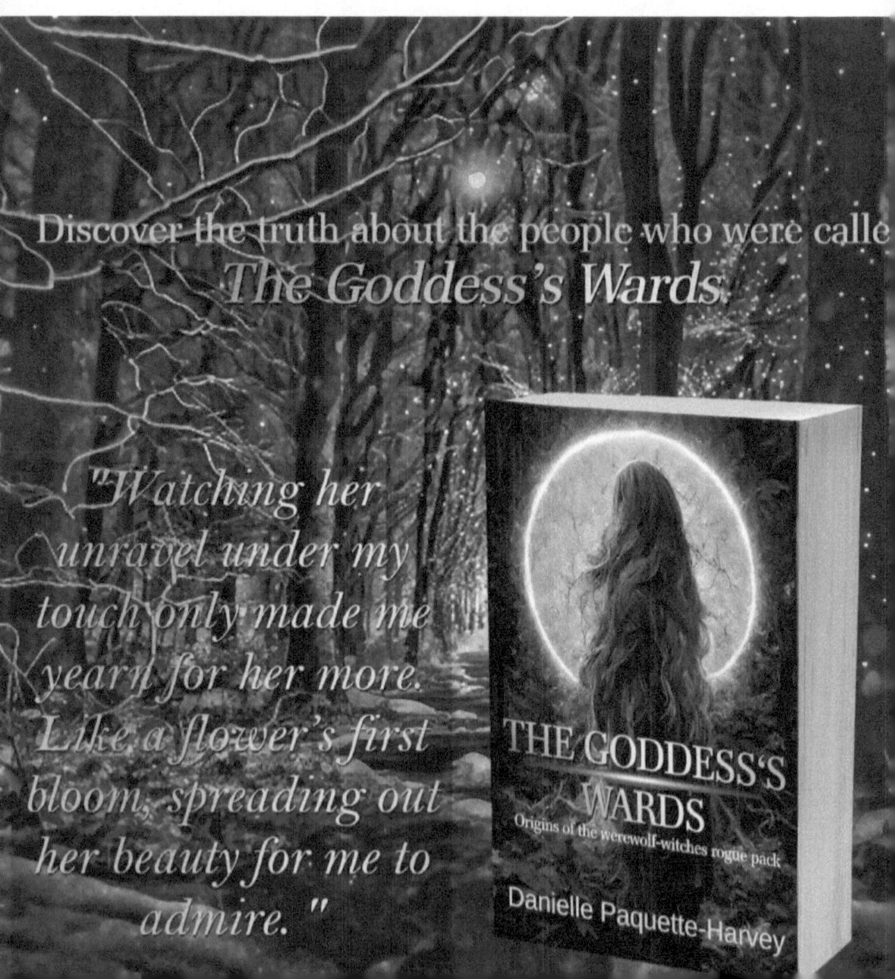

Thank you

I wanted to take some time to thank everyone who's been helping and supporting me. I know I will forget some people and feel bad about it. Obviously, I can't name everyone because it would take several pages.

First off, I need to thank my husband Martin, and my kids, Catherine and William, for their patience and support in this big adventure. They have been patient with me, while I've been spending my evenings and weekends writing. Always rooting for me, trying to help me in any way they can. I love you very dearly, with all my heart, and will always love you.

I also need to thank some of my closest friends, Julie, Georgie, and Stephane. I have known you guys for years. I know you are amongst my biggest fans. I always appreciate you and even though we might not see each other as often as we'd like, you are always in my heart.

I also want to thank everyone else in my family, many of my friends and colleagues from work, and also my neighbors, that read and support me. Love you guys! I know some of you didn't even read in English before. I'm so grateful you chose to read my book as your first book in English.

Now, over the months I've become an author, I have met loads of great people from all around the world. I can truly say that friendship knows no boundaries. I am lucky to say that I speak with people in Australia, Malaysia, United Kingdom, the United States, and India daily, and I have friends all over the world.

I really need to thank Chelsea. She's my twin sister from another country. Sincerely, in the short amount of time I've known you, you've become one of my closest friends. I'm so grateful to have met you. Thanks for all your love and support.

I really want to thank my friend Charles as well. You are an amazing friend. I truly enjoy our conversations, your support, and friendship. Even with the difference in time zones, you've also become one of my closest friends. One day I'll cross the ocean to visit you. Ciao la banane table!

I want to thank you all, all my friends around the world. I would love to mention all of you, but it would be way too long to name everyone. I hope you all know how much I appreciate you. Even if you're so far away that when it's Sunday for me, it's already Monday morning for you. Even if covid makes it that there's no postage service from my country to yours. Even if you live on a tiny island where it's always rainy. You guys are amazing, and I wouldn't be there if it wasn't for each and every one of you.

Thank you from the bottom of my heart!

To many more years together!

Danielle

www.ingramcontent.com/pod-product-compliance
Lightning Source LLC
Chambersburg PA
CBHW051322190726
48290CB00001B/274